'You must move in exclusively female circles.'

Ben's lids lowered as he re-appraised her.

She decided to turn the tables on him, and, leaning back in her chair, Maggie turned half towards him and studied him openly. 'How old are *you*, Dr Bradshaw?'

'Ben. I'm thirty-one.'

'Single?'

'So far.'

She let her eyes trail slowly over his body. 'You must move in exclusively male circles,' she murmured.

Dear Reader

RAW DEAL is second in Caroline Anderson's trilogy, in which Maggie is manipulated by her grandmother into discovering appearances can deceive. We go to Australia for Lilian Darcy's A PRIVATE ARRANGEMENT, where Belinda Jones cares for a pregnant diabetic—problems! Clare Mackay unfolds SISTER PENNY'S SECRET, in her second novel, and Elizabeth Petty returns with THE SURGEON FROM FRANCE, where a delightful old patient plays matchmaker. Have fun!

The Editor

Caroline Anderson's nursing career was brought to an abrupt halt by a back injury, but her interest in medical things led her to work first as a medical secretary, and then, after completing her teacher training, as a lecturer in medical office practice to trainee medical secretaries. In addition to writing, she also runs her own business from her home in rural Suffolk, where she lives with her husband, two daughters, mother and dog.

Recent titles by the same author:

A PERFECT HERO
PLAYING THE JOKER (first in the trilogy)

RAW DEAL

BY

CAROLINE ANDERSON

MILLS & BOON LIMITED
ETON HOUSE   18–24 PARADISE ROAD
RICHMOND   SURREY   TW9 1SR

Thanks to Gill, Juno and Mary-Jo.
This one's for Kiki,
who knows all about raw deals.

*First published in Great Britain 1993
by Mills & Boon Limited*

© Caroline Anderson 1993

*Australian copyright 1993
Philippine copyright 1993
This edition 1993*

ISBN 0 263 77980 7

*Set in 10 on 10½ pt Linotron Plantin
03-9301-49744*

*Typeset in Great Britain by Centracet, Cambridge
Made and printed in Great Britain*

CHAPTER ONE

'SHE's up to something, you know—have I told you the latest?'

Jo's lips twitched at her friend's outraged tone. 'Which particular latest?'

Maggie Wells straightened from the incubator and grinned wryly.

'Lucinda's not going on the cruise. Says she thinks her health isn't up to it—something about lassitude and being very run down.'

'Maybe she is?'

Maggie snorted. 'Lucinda? That old rascal's as strong as an ox. She doesn't know the meaning of the word lassitude! She's on more committees than I've had hot dinners, and if she isn't arranging the flowers in the cathedral she's at some RMBF lunch party or else hatching my nuptials with her cronies. No, if I know my grandmother, there's something sinister behind it, and I'll give you three guesses what!'

'You could always give in and marry one of these eligible young men——'

'Are you kidding? I neither want nor need Lucinda's help to find a husband. I'm quite capable of doing it on my own.'

'Are you? When did you last go out for a serious date with a man you wanted to be with?'

Maggie met Jo's eyes with habitual honesty. 'I'm not sure I ever have, but one thing I am sure of—

5

my grandmother isn't any better at finding my Mr Right than I am!'

She jotted a reading down on the baby's chart, and smiled at Jo. 'Amy's improving.'

They both looked at the baby, still unbelievably tiny but stronger with every day that passed. Her young, tragically drug-addicted mother had committed suicide the day after her birth, leaving a note putting the baby in Jo's care. All that remained was to convince the Social Services that Jo and her new husband Alex were suitable adoptive parents—and that was by no means a foregone conclusion.

'How are the adoption proceedings going?' Maggie asked now, and Jo shrugged and gave a strained smile.

'Slow, intrusive, very thorough. They have to be, don't they? After all, Amy's the important one.'

Maggie nodded. 'I hope—you know. . .'

'Yes—thanks, Maggie.' She glanced at her watch. 'Have you got time for a quick coffee? I promised Annie I'd meet her at eleven.'

'It'll have to be a quick one.'

They left the quiet bustle of the special care baby unit and made their way down in the lift.

As the doors opened they met Alex Carter, Jo's husband, and he dropped a kiss on Jo's lips and smiled. 'Ships in the night—how's Amy?'

'Better.'

'Great—I'll try and pop up later. Must go—I've got an emergency section. I don't suppose you've got time to assist, Jo?'

'Well—as it's you. . .!' She grinned at Maggie. 'Duty calls, I'm afraid.'

Maggie watched as the lift doors slid shut on them,

Jo tall and slender with enviable curves and a wild mane of dark red hair, Alex taller still, and good-looking in a soberly distinguished sort of way. Sober, that was, until you caught the way he looked at his wife.

Maggie felt an unexpected pang of envy. For all she complained about her grandmother's conniving and matchmaking, she would love nothing more than to settle down with the right man.

She sighed. Perhaps she was just too darned fussy?

She found Anne Gabriel in the canteen, and explained that Jo had had to assist Alex with an emergency.

Anne nodded. 'I just admitted her. Antepartum haemorrhage. If all goes well, you'll have another baby upstairs to deal with.'

Maggie dropped into the low chair and sipped her coffee. 'They'll be a few minutes yet. I'd better make the most of it.'

'They look happy, don't they?' Anne said after a moment, and Maggie noticed that she looked wistful.

She gave a tiny, humourless laugh. 'Yes, they do. I was just envying them a minute ago.'

Anne smiled. 'Me too. Never mind, perhaps you'll meet someone on this cruise—where are you going?'

'Singapore and the Indonesian Islands—except I don't think I am. My grandmother's pulled out—says she's ill.'

'Oh, dear! Anything serious?'

Maggie snorted. 'You jest. No, she's up to something. I expect the captain is the emotionally crippled son of one of her bridge partners!'

Anne laughed. 'Anyway, why does that stop you going?'

'Well, I can't go without her—she's paid for my ticket so that I can accompany her. It wouldn't be moral——'

Anne stared at her in amazement. 'Are you nuts? She's loaded! She could pay for that cruise out of her small change! I think you should go—she obviously intends you to.'

'That,' Maggie said wryly, 'is what bothers me.' She sipped her coffee again, and then met Anne's eyes over the top of the cup. 'Of course, it's always possible that she really *is* sick. . . Perhaps I'll go and see her.'

'You do that—on the way to the airport! And if you decide not to go, give me a shout. I'll take your ticket any day. I could cope with a week of luxury in the Far East!'

'Ten days.'

'Even better!'

Just then Maggie's bleep went, and with a resigned sigh she put down her coffee. 'I'll keep you posted,' she promised, and made her way over to the wall phone.

'Dr Wells—you bleeped me.'

'Oh, yes, Dr Wells, you're wanted in Obstetric Theatre Two, please,' the switchboard operator told her.

Maggie arrived in Theatre to find Alex and Jo just about to deliver the premature baby whose mother had had an antepartum haemorrhage.

'Do we know the gestational age?' she asked.

'Twenty-six weeks,' Alex said tersely, 'and he doesn't look any too large.'

As she was handed the tiny slippery mite, she bit her lip and frowned.

'It's going to be touch and go—he looks pretty flat,' she said to no one in particular. 'Let's get him sucked out and get some oxygen into him, and I think he's going to need surfactant. Could somebody call Peter Travers?'

Behind her she was conscious of Alex's quiet requests and directions, and Jo's calm response as they struggled to control the haemorrhage.

'That's more like it,' Alex murmured, and Maggie felt the atmosphere lift a little. 'How's the baby?'

She shrugged. 'Iffy. I'm doing what I can.'

'It's all we can do,' Alex said steadyingly, continuing his fight for the mother.

Peter Travers, the head of Maggie's firm, came into the room and took one look at the baby before shaking his head.

'This one's going to be all uphill,' he muttered, warming his stethoscope and running it over the baby's chest. 'He's got a murmur—it may settle.' His voice was devoid of hope. 'Right, let's get him into SCBU and wire him up. He's got this far, you never know.'

But he didn't make it, and it was Maggie who was with the little boy and his father when he died. His mother had seen him and held him briefly when she came round, but her condition was still very weak and, apart from Maggie, the baby's father was the only one there when he slipped qietly away.

Mr Grainger lifted his eyes to Maggie's, and they were dazed with shock and pain. 'He's gone. . .' he whispered.

'I'm so sorry,' Maggie said heavily, and, opening

the incubator, she lifted out the tiny body and placed it in the man's arms, and then she held him and cried with him as he cradled his tiny son.

'Nicky'll be heartbroken,' he said gruffly, and his voice cracked.

'Yes, she will,' Maggie told him gently. 'She'll need time to come to terms with it. I'll ask Mr Carter if he thinks she's strong enough to be told, but on the whole it's best not to drag out her hopes for long. I expect she'll want to hold him again while he's still warm, and we'll take photographs of him, and keep his clothes for you so you'll be able to remember him.'

The man looked worried. 'Is that a good idea? All those reminders?'

Maggie nodded. 'You won't need reminders, Mr Grainger. You'll both think of him often, and he'll always be real to you. He is real. Memories can be a great comfort, and we try and give you as many memories as we can to take with you.'

'What will they do with—with him?'

Maggie brushed the tiny baby's cheek with her knuckle. 'He'll be taken to the mortuary, and any time you or your wife want to see him you only have to ask and you can hold him if you want, as many times as you need to, and then, when you're ready, he'll have a funeral just like anybody else.'

'They don't. . .incinerate. . .?'

Maggie shook her head, understanding his fears. 'No. He's a person, just like any other person. His death is just as real, just as important as anyone else's. Remember that. You have a right to your grief, and to proper recognition of his short life. Did he have a name?'

Mr Grainger swallowed hard. 'Samuel.'

'That's a lovely name. He's a beautiful baby.'

Samuel's father cradled the tiny body against his chest. 'Yes, he is, isn't he?' His voice, for all its sadness, was full of wonder. He turned to Maggie. 'Thank you for explaining——'

She shook her head helplessly. 'You're welcome. Do you want to be alone with him for a while?'

He nodded blindly.

'I'll phone Mr Carter.'

She walked quickly away, took a second to compose herself and picked up the phone. Alex was on the ward and came up immediately, sparing her a quick squeeze on the shoulder.

'Sorry—it's awful, isn't it?' he said quietly.

Maggie left him dealing with the man and made her way into Amy's cubicle. Because of the possibility that she had been contaminated with the HIV virus by her mother, Amy was nursed in isolation, and it gave Maggie the solitude she needed to pull herself together.

At least this was one baby who was beginning to respond to treatment. She had stopped twitching, and now at five weeks old she was breathing independently, beginning to suck for herself and was nearly ready to go home. No doubt once Christmas was over she would be allocated to a foster mother until her adoption was decided. Maggie just hoped that the woman would be flexible and receptive to Jo, because she was going to have a hell of a fight on her hands if she intended to keep them apart!

As if her thoughts had produced her from thin air, Jo appeared behind Maggie and touched her shoulder gently.

'OK, Maggie?' she asked softly.

Maggie sniffed. 'Yes. Just—it's such a waste.'

Jo nodded. 'You win some, you lose some. Are you off duty?'

'Yes—I think I'll go and tackle my grandmother on the subject of her suddenly precarious health.'

Jo chuckled. 'Good idea. Give her my love.'

'Not until I've strangled her!' she replied with a strained laugh. 'See you tomorrow.'

She drove her little VW Polo back to her flat, the converted middle floor of a Victorian pile in the old part of town, and, running upstairs, she lit the gas fire, kicked off her shoes and let down her long red-gold hair before picking up the phone and settling comfortably in the armchair by the fire.

'Lucinda? Hi—it's Maggie. How are you?'

'Oh, Margaret, darling, how lovely to hear from you. I'll be all right—just a little weak, that's all, darling. Don't worry about me.'

Maggie twiddled the flex of the phone, winding her finger into the coils. 'I thought I'd come and see you——'

'Oh, no, goodness, dear! That would never do! I think it's a touch of flu, actually, and that's positively the *last* thing you need with all those tiny babies you come in contact with. No, no, dear, you stay away, do you understand?'

Maggie's lips twisted into a wry smile.

'I understand, Grannie, darling.'

'Don't call me that, dear—so ageing! Anyway, now, are you all set to go?'

Old fraud, Maggie thought fondly. There wasn't a trace of a fluey cough or sniff, and she sounded about as weak as a barracuda.

'Yes, I'm all set, but I don't think I should go without you——'

'Nonsense! You need a holiday, darling, more than I do. You must go, otherwise I shall feel obliged to drag myself out of my sick bed and accompany you, and God knows what that'll do to my precarious health!'

'God knows!' Maggie agreed drily. 'Anyway, I could do with some company later—maybe I will drop in just for a short while—I promise to keep out of your way so I won't catch anything.'

'No! No, Margaret, you mustn't! I simply forbid it!' her grandmother all but shrieked, then, collecting herself almost audibly, she continued in a noticeably weaker voice, 'Anyway, darling, I thought I'd have an early night. What was it you wanted to see me about?'

Your interview for RADA, Maggie thought ruefully, and then remembered.

'Oh, nothing drastic. I just had a rotten day.'

She told her grandmother all about Samuel Grainger, and Lucinda tutted and ooed and oh, deared and made all the right noises.

'You must have a holiday, darling,' she ended, 'otherwise you'll get dreadfully depressed and you'll get wrinkles. So ageing. You go.'

'Yes, Grannie,' she replied, and cut off the protest with a kiss. 'I'll try and pop over on Christmas Day if not before, but anyway I'll come and see you before I leave,' she promised.

In fact she didn't get a chance before Christmas Day, and even then she was working.

Christmas Day on the paediatric wards was hectic from start to finish, the normal routine squeezed into half the time to allow for the obligatory merry-making, with Peter Travers dressed up as Father Christmas and Maggie forced to play the Fairy Godmother in a little panto they put on in the afternoon.

She finally got away at seven o'clock in the evening for a short while, and, without even stopping to change out of her working clothes, she drove the short distance to the smart side of town and pulled up outside her grandmother's house. There were lights blazing in all the downstairs rooms, and a very new-looking Mercedes dominated the drive. She squeezed in behind it and, picking up the parcel which contained some very lacy and extremely ungrandmotherly underwear, Maggie slipped out of the car and walked up to the front window. Peering in, she saw her grandmother dancing with a tall, distinguished-looking man in his seventies, at a guess, and remarkably good-looking for his age.

They were obviously alone, and totally absorbed in each other's company. Mesmerised, Maggie watched her grandmother flirt outrageously with her handsome escort.

Her head was thrown back, and even through the glass Maggie could hear the light ripple of coquettish laughter emanating from Lucinda's enviably well-preserved throat—a throat Maggie was tempted to wrap her fingers round and squeeze firmly!

The lousy old fraud! she thought crossly, and then hesitated, her hand raised to rap on the glass. Why not go along with her? She might not be ill now, but she was getting on, and plotting the romantic downfall of Maggie's spinsterhood was one of the greatest pleasures of her old age.

'Oh, hell, how can it hurt to allow her her fun?' Maggie muttered. 'And she's right—I do need a holiday.'

So she rang the doorbell, cheerfully wished a Merry Christmas to the tall stranger who opened the door, kissed her grandmother solicitously on the cheek, pretended not to notice the slightly height-ened colour or the litter of sherry glasses, and perched beside Lucinda on the couch, eyeing her thoughtfully.

'You do look a little peaky, darling—and a bit breathless. Perhaps you're right—it's a long flight.'

'But you will go without me, won't you?'

Maggie stifled her smile. 'Yes, I'll go. I expect there'll be a lot of boring old fuddy-duddies, but perhaps there'll be some nice young officer to cheer me up,' she said naughtily.

She inadvertently intercepted the look her grand-mother and the stranger exchanged, and fiddled with the present to cover her sudden need to laugh. That stage wink! So he was in on it, too, was he?

'Is that for me?'

'Yes—saucy undies. Happy Christmas, darling.'

'Oh, Margaret, how sweet—Gerald, pass me that envelope from the mantelpiece, would you?' She pressed it into Maggie's hand. 'Just a little spending money and your ticket—have a lovely time.'

'I will. Bless you. I'll take lots of photos. And Grannie,' she admonished, 'you haven't introduced me to your guest.'

'How rude of me! Darling, this is Gerald Palmer, an old friend from simply years ago. . .' She waved her hand to indicate possibly several decades—or

even centuries. 'Gerald, my granddaughter,
Margaret——'

'Maggie,' Maggie corrected.

'Enchanted, my dear,' Mr Palmer murmured as
he took her hand and lifted it to his lips. 'So like
your grandmother at your age—I would have known
you anywhere.'

Well, no wonder she looks a little breathless!
Maggie thought as she excused herself and left them
to continue their merrymaking. The man overflowed
with charm. She instantly forgave him his part in the
conspiracy—and her grandmother. They were probably helpless to defend themselves against each
other! But she did rather wonder about his part in it
all. . .

Dawn was just breaking over the sea as the
Singapore Airlines flight touched down in Changi
Airport. It was the thirtieth of December, and
England was in the grip of a sudden, biting freeze.

As Maggie stepped from the plane and lifted her
face to the sun, she was flooded with warmth and a
sudden, unexpected surge of excitement.

The last week had been hectic and exhausting,
and she was so tired after the previous eighteen
months that she had slept right through the flight.
Now it seemed as if she had woken to a dream
world.

Once in the terminal building, she retrieved her
luggage, and, after clearing Customs, referred to her
instructions and proceeded to the allocated rendez-
vous point.

There her party was warmly welcomed by a young
ship's officer, who checked them all off on a list,

ensured that they all had their luggage and then shepherded them to a waiting coach.

Then they were whisked in air-conditioned comfort along the East Coast Parkway past the glorious profusion of vast banks of bougainvillaeas, over the harbour bridges under the lee of the towering skyscrapers to the World Trade Centre harbour, and were very soon ensconced aboard the *Island Pearl*, their home for the next ten days.

Looking around her, Maggie decided that it was certainly sumptuous without being in the least bit tacky, and small enough for a definitely family feel. Her grandmother would have enjoyed it, Maggie thought with a pang, but then reminded herself that it was entirely her own fault she was missing it.

She was shown to her cabin, a surprisingly spacious twin down on the Java deck—by a freak of fate, she thought, on the same deck as the medical centre. There and then she vowed to tell no one that she was a doctor, or she'd be hounded by the malingerers if she so much as emerged from her cabin and caught them in search of the ship's MO.

The cabin, she noted, was blissfully cool. Even this early the air outside was hot, and given time would soar into the eighties or nineties.

She peered through the porthole and saw a flotilla of little fishing vessels and small yachts milling about in the harbour. Fascinated, she propped her chin on her hand and watched for several minutes, until the public address system 'ting-tonged' into life.

'Ladies and gentlemen,' a well-modulated female voice began, 'welcome aboard the *Island Pearl*. If you would care to make your way to the Malacca deck in half an hour where a buffet breakfast is awaiting you, the captain and crew will be pleased to meet you and give you details of the entertainments and facilities available for your enjoyment during your cruise with us. A map of the ship is posted by each companionway, and another copy is in each cabin by the door. We look forward to your company.'

Ting-tong.

Maggie realised that she was starving. Investigating the doors in her cabin, she found a little shower-room and a wardrobe. Hot, sticky and travel-weary, she had just stripped and was standing under the shower when there was a tap on the door.

'Your luggage, madam,' a voice said, and a suitcase appeared in the cabin.

'Perfect timing,' she said with satisfaction, and, towelling herself dry, she opened the case and studied the contents.

Not being spoilt for choice, she pulled out a cotton jersey T-shirt dress in pansy-blue that almost exactly matched her eyes, and slipped her feet into cotton sandals.

Tying back her damp hair into a pony-tail with a big fabric band, she brushed on a lick of lipstick and smiled falsely at herself.

Good grief! she thought. I'm nervous. How ridiculous.

With that she opened her cabin door, locked it behind her and made her way up to the Malacca deck.

She was eyeing the buffet and wishing Lucinda was with her after all when a sprightly woman in her sixties smiled at her.

'Dazzling choice, isn't it? I'm Rhoda. How do you do?'

Maggie took the proffered hand. 'Maggie. I'm pleased to meet you.' And she was, she realised, relaxing almost visibly. 'Are you alone too?'

'Yes—which is understandable. But you should have some gorgeous young thing in tow—how about the first officer? He's spectacularly handsome if you like the Latin type. Bit short, but then you aren't tall. Or one of the others—I saw the perfect man a little while ago. I do so love men in uniform, don't you, dear? So romantic, somehow. . .'

Maggie laughingly restrained her. 'Please, Rhoda! I've been working very hard and I'm here to rest. The last thing I need is a romance.'

'Rubbish! Everybody needs romance! It's the most revitalising thing in the world. Now let me see . . .'

Maggie eyed her new companion warily. 'You don't by any chance know my grandmother, do you? Lucinda Wells.'

'Lucinda Wells—no, I can't say I do, darling. Why?'

Maggie shrugged ruefully. 'Oh, nothing. You just reminded me of her.'

Rhoda threw back her head and let out a rippling tinkle of laughter. 'Oh, dear, excuse me. . . Is she trying to marry you off, poppet?'

'You could say that!'

Rhoda patted her hand. 'Can't say I blame her. You're far too pretty to let loose on the streets alone. I'd want you settled, too.'

But despite the constant roving of Rhoda's eyes during breakfast in the Frangipani Room and the

more formal welcome that followed it in the Penang
Lounge, the perfect man remained mercifully
invisible.

Shortly after the captain finished his welcoming
speech, the ship's engines thrummed gently to life
and she pulled slowly out of harbour and began the
lazy cruise down the Java Sea to Bali.

Rhoda went to scout out the sunbeds, and Maggie,
glad of a little peace, explored the ship until lunch.

The afternoon found her under a sunshade with a
book, enjoying the feel of the light breeze over her
skin as the little ship cruised steadily down towards
the equator. Despite the lazy day she felt ready for
bed, a fact enhanced by the change in the time. Of
course, it was in reality long past her normal bed-
time, but before she could make her escape there
was dinner to get through, and she found to her
confusion that there was to be no escape. Her
company was requested at the captain's table.

When the ting-tong of the PA called them for
dinner, Maggie looked at the two formal dresses she
had brought, eenie-meenie-minie-moed and ended
up with the midnight silk jersey.

She piled her hair into a loose heap on her head,
teased out a few tendrils and twirled in front of the
mirror.

What she saw was enough to send her scurrying
back to the wardrobe, but bearing in mind that she
would have to wear both dresses in the end there
seemed little point in changing. It was just that, in
the shop and with Jo and Annie egging her on, it
hadn't seemed quite so. . . Oh, well. Who was going
to see, anyway? After all, she'd already seen the
captain, and he was a widower in his late fifties with

grey, thinning hair and undoubtedly a wallet full of family snaps he would pull out at the first opportunity! Perhaps she'd misjudged her grandmother after all?

She was the last but one to arrive at the captain's table, and apologised slightly breathlessly for her lateness.

'Nonsense, my dear,' Captain Rodrigues said jovially. 'We're still waiting for one member of the party—ah, here he is. Ben, come and join us!'

'I do apologise for being late,' a deep, rich voice murmured from behind her. 'One of the penalties of the medical profession.'

As he slid gracefully into the seat beside her, Maggie caught a glimpse of fair hair, blue eyes and a boyish grin above a crisp white dress uniform with gold braid and a red cross on the breast pocket before she lowered her eyes.

Bingo. The ship's doctor. And that explained the siting of her cabin next to the medical centre.

She wasn't sure whether to laugh or cry.

CHAPTER TWO

'Now you're all here, let me introduce you,' the captain was saying, but the only name Maggie heard was that of the ship's doctor—and he was called Bradshaw, not Palmer, which blew her newly formed theory that he might be Gerald's son! Perhaps it was just coincidence that such an eligible man had suddenly appeared at her side?

Her mind fell over laughing at the very idea. Where Lucinda was involved, coincidences simply didn't happen—they were ruthlessly arranged. And anyway, there was still the question of the strategic positioning of her cabin.

Stifling the urge to laugh, Maggie looked up and encountered a boyish grin under a straight, slightly aquiline nose. She wondered if he was in on the conspiracy. He bowed slightly towards her.

'Miss Wells,' he murmured. 'Welcome to the *Island Pearl*. What do you think of the old bucket so far?'

Maggie smiled. So what if it was all set up? She might as well have some fun. 'She's lovely—I think I'm really going to enjoy it.'

'We shall see that you do,' Captain Rodrigues interrupted. 'I'm sure Dr Bradshaw would be delighted to keep you company—Miss Wells's grandmother was to have accompanied her, Ben, but at the last minute she became unwell.'

'How unfortunate,' the doctor said smoothly. 'I'll

have to see if I can't step into her shoes, at least for part of the time.'

'I'd rather you didn't,' Maggie told him with a laugh. 'She's forever trying to marry me off!'

One eyebrow quirked above his extraordinary grey-blue eyes. 'Really? I wouldn't have thought that would be very difficult.' His eyes travelled lazily over the contours of Maggie's figure, lovingly revealed by the sensuous drape of the midnight-blue silk jersey.

She shifted uncomfortably, forced a bright smile and met his eyes challengingly. 'I'm extremely picky,' she told him frankly.

A slow smile lit his eyes. 'You can afford to be. After all, you've got plenty of time—how old are you? Twenty-one? Twenty-two, maybe?'

'I'm twenty-eight—not that it's any of your business,' she retorted, irritated that she should feel flattered by his implication of immaturity. Perhaps Lucinda's constant exhortation not to do or think anything ageing was rubbing off on her?

'You must move in exclusively female circles,' he said, and his lids lowered as he reappraised her.

She decided to turn the tables on him, and, leaning back in her chair, she turned half towards him and studied him openly.

'How old are you, Dr Bradshaw?'

'Ben. I'm thirty-one.'

'Single?'

'So far.'

'Any—er—commitments?'

His lips twitched. 'Not at the moment.'

She let her eyes trail slowly over his body. 'You

must move in exclusively male circles,' she murmured.

He gave a short, appreciative laugh.

'*Touché*.' He raised his glass to her in a silent toast, and sipped the smooth red wine before setting the glass down and turning his attention back to her. 'So, Miss Wells——'

'Maggie.'

'Maggie. What do you do to occupy your time when you aren't gallivanting around the world with or without your matchmaking grandparent?'

She chuckled. 'I work with children,' she told him, half truthfully.

'A teacher?'

'No—I work in a hospital, actually.'

'A nurse?'

'No—I——'

'Occupational therapist? Physio?'

She thought of the endless hours on duty, sometimes as many as a hundred and twenty hours a week. 'Dogsbody, really,' she replied with a tinge of bitter irony.

'I'm sure they love you,' he said, and she was surprised at the sincerity in his voice. 'You have an openness, a frank honesty; kids like that.'

She thought of some of the painful procedures it was often her duty to perform, and shook her head. 'I don't know if they love me, but I do my best for them. It isn't always enough.'

She glanced up and surprised a look of pain that twisted his features briefly.

'No,' he replied quietly. 'It isn't always enough, and sometimes it's too much.'

She was saved from an inane reply by the arrival of the first course, a delicious hors-d'oeuvre.

She made her selection and nibbled the smoked salmon trout thoughtfully. So, her lightweight, play-boy doctor had hidden depths, did he? Even more important, then, that she should keep a distance from him, because, while she could easily talk her-self out of falling for an emotional lightweight, she had the uneasy feeling that for all his flirting Ben Bradshaw was anything but, and if they found too much common ground—well, it could be a disaster. She speared a king prawn with more force than was strictly necessary.

Maggie was no fool. She knew she was ripe for picking, but, having escaped the somewhat fumbled clutches of her generation of medical students, she was in no hurry now to hurl herself at the first half-decent man who came along—especially not one who was apparently in hiding from some demon in his past.

A hundred years ago, she mused, he might have joined the Foreign Legion. Now he was condemned to dishing out Kwells to pampered old ladies and bandaging the occasional twisted ankle resulting from an over-enthusiastic game of deck quoits!

And yet, despite her determination to keep her distance, as the food came and went and conver-sation ebbed and flowed around her, she found her glance straying to his face, and her thoughts straying to his words. She wondered what might have hap-pened when his best had obviously been too much, and thought again of little Samuel Grainger whose fight had been so brief, and for whom her best had fallen a long way short of the mark.

'Penny for them?'

She glanced quickly up, and saw that, above his smile, his eyes were concerned, as if her face had revealed too much. She shook her head. 'Sorry, I was miles away. So tell me, Ben, what do I have to look forward to in the next few days?'

He laughed and eased back in his chair. 'Almost anything. What would you like to do tonight—a quiet drink in the bar, flirting with Lady Luck in the casino, a film, or something romantic—dancing on deck in the moonlight, with the wind in your hair and the bright gleam of the phosphorescence leaving a sparkling trail in our wake?'

His voice had softened and deepened, and she was caught in the magnetic snare of his eyes, unable to look away.

'That sounds almost too good to be true,' she found herself saying, and then everyone was rising from the table and she was taking Ben's arm, aware with every cell in her body of the sinuous strength of his muscles under the fine, soft wool of his white dress uniform.

They collected a drink from the bar and made their way out on deck. All around them people were talking softly and the air was filled with the tinkle of laughter and ice in glasses, murmured voices and sighs of delight.

They found a gap at the rail and stood together, and, due either to the slight motion of the ship or the unaccustomed alcohol, Maggie found herself swaying gently against his tall, hard body.

Ben took her empty glass and put it down, then grinned at her. 'Come on,' he whispered. 'Perk of the job—I know somewhere quiet!'

They threaded their way through the laughing crowd, up a companionway and through a little gate marked 'Authorised Personnel Only', then they were out on the bows, watching the phosphorus turn the water a ghostly green as the ship sliced through the sea.

The hum of the engines and the splash of water drowned out the music and laughter they had left behind, and Ben moved up beside Maggie, wrapping his arm around her waist and easing her up against his side. The heat of the day was gone, and in the cooling breeze she was glad of the warmth of his body. The weight of his arm seemed so natural, so right, somehow. She relaxed against him and breathed deeply of the tropic night.

The air was rich with the salt tang of the sea and the smell of fresh paint, and every now and again she caught a glimpse of a flying fish leaping from the water, the phosphorescence trailing behind it like a tiny comet.

'What a beautiful night,' she sighed, and Ben's arm tightened as he turned her into his embrace.

His face was sharply etched in the moonlight, and she watched the emotions play across it as he slowly pulled out her hairpins and shook her hair loose.

'Absolutely beautiful,' he murmured in response, and she knew in that second that he was going to kiss her.

I ought to run! she thought, but instead she tipped back her head to make it easier for him, and waited, fascinated, as his firm, full lips lowered and brushed against hers, teasing her with tiny, sipping kisses until her trembling sigh broke through his control and he threaded his fingers through her hair and steadied her against the onslaught of his mouth.

After what seemed like forever and yet wasn't nearly long enough, he lifted his head and folded her against his chest, her head tucked neatly under his chin against the wild beating of his heart.

He held her there until his heart had slowed, and then he let her go, moving away to stand by the guard rail, his hands braced on the teak top rail, his head bowed.

'We shouldn't have done that,' she said breathlessly, wondering if her legs would collapse without his support, and he lifted his head and met her eyes with a rueful grin.

'You're undoubtedly right, but I'm not going to apologise. You're beautiful, Maggie, with your mermaid's hair flowing round your shoulders and your eyes wide and innocent—they're the colour of crushed pansies, did you know that? And your clear, pale skin—you'll have to be careful not to burn.' His finger trailed slowly over her bare shoulder and down her arm. 'It would be a tragedy to mark that exquisite perfection.'

'Has anybody ever told you you've got the smooth tongue of an Irishman?' Maggie asked drily, to cover the wild leap of her heart.

Ben chuckled. 'Just a natural ladies' man,' he said easily. 'Come on, let me escort you back to the happy throng, then I must go and hand out more seasick pills. I saw a wave a moment ago—no doubt I'll be the most popular man on board before long.'

His voice was tinged with irony, and Maggie looked up at him, catching a flash of discontent on his face.

'Don't you ever long to be involved in mainstream medicine again?' she asked, and wasn't surprised when his face went carefully blank.

'Not often. It's a wonderful life here, you know. Sun, sea, sand—even the occasional mermaid thrown in for good measure!'

She wasn't fooled. 'It sounds wonderful for a holiday, but I would have thought after a while it would be extremely boring.'

He gave a funny, twisted little laugh. 'It has its moments. Come on, I'm afraid I really do have to go and see to my patients.'

As they made their way back across the sun-bleached deck that gleamed strangely white in the moonlight, Maggie felt suddenly very tired.

'I think, actually, I'll turn in now if you don't mind. I've got rather a headache.'

'It's jet lag,' he told her. 'You'll be all right in the morning.'

On the way back through the Penang Lounge, Rhoda spotted them and winked broadly. Oh, good grief, whatever would she think? And it would be worse if she watched them disappear together! Maggie, blushing slightly, turned to Ben and stopped him with a hand on his arm.

'There's someone I must have a word with. Thank you for—this evening.'

'You're welcome,' he murmured, a smile playing in the corners of his eyes. 'Can you find your way back to your cabin?'

'I'm sure I will. Goodnight, Ben.'

'Goodnight, my little mermaid. See you tomorrow.'

He turned away, and Maggie looked up to see Rhoda weaving her way across the room.

'That's him—the perfect man—absolutely splendid! How did you find him?'

Maggie shrugged and laughed. 'I was sitting next to him for dinner. He's the ship's doctor. He's been very—charming.'

Rhoda eyed her quizzically. 'And did his charm smudge your lipstick and tumble your hair down over your shoulders and leave you looking so alive?'

Maggie flushed and lowered her eyes, and Rhoda laughed softly and patted her hand.

'You enjoy it,' she advised. 'A little romance will do you the power of good.'

'Yes, well, just now I feel like ten hours' sleep. I'll see you tomorrow.'

She made her way down to her cabin on Java Deck, taking the stairs as the lifts were all busy. Her mind on the magic of Ben's kiss and the lingering feel of his hands in her hair, she lost her footing and tumbled inelègantly to the deck, landing with a soft cry.

'You didn't have to throw yourself at my feet,' a familiar voice murmured. 'A word would have been enough.'

'Ouch,' she muttered crossly. 'Don't fool around, Ben, I've hurt my ankle.'

'Let me see,' he said in a soothing voice, and carefully eased her leg straight. 'It doesn't seem too bad—let's get you on to your bed and have a closer look. Where's your cabin?'

She showed him the key, and he hoisted her effortlessly into his arms and carried her down the corridor.

'Good job it's not far,' she joked, 'I'd hate to put your back out!'

He laughed. 'You weigh practically nothing,' he told her. 'We'll have to see if we can't get some flesh on your bones in the next few days.'

Oh, hell, she thought, that's all it is. A few days. She wished she weren't so headily conscious of the lingering scent of cologne that drifted towards her on his body's warmth. His jaw was inches from her face, and she could see the faint trace of stubble roughening the skin. Her fingers itched to rasp against the slightly coarse texture, to feel the roughness of his jaw graze her skin as he trailed hot, lazy kisses down her throat——

'Here we are—can you open the door?'

Jet lag! she thought, and wriggled round in his arms to put the key in the lock and turn it.

'I'm sure I can walk,' she said belatedly.

'I'm sure you can, but until I've checked your ankle I've got a good excuse to hold you!' he replied with a laugh, setting her down gently on one of the bunks.

'Take your tights off,' he told her, and turned away while she self-consciously wriggled out of them and tucked them under her pillow.

'OK,' she said, and he turned back and perched on the edge of the bunk, taking her ankle firmly but gently in his hands and rotating it carefully, studying her face as he did so.

She winced, and he nodded and put it down, much to her relief. His hands were cool and firm and very masculine, and she felt suddenly terribly conscious of his presence in her cabin. He was bigger than she had realised, not taller, but more solid, somehow.

He had shed his jacket and was wearing a crisp white shirt and tie, and his shoulders looked broader and very menacing—as menacing, that was, as he could manage to look with that little-boy grin and the wicked twinkle in his eye!

'You'll have to take it easy for a day or so—plenty of rest, all right?'

A little imp frolicked in her eyes. 'I was going to dance till four in the morning, jog round the deck to clear my head, then play deck quoits till lunchtime.'

He smiled, slowly and wickedly. 'If you don't promise to be sensible I'll have to lash you to the bed.'

'That'll make it very difficult for you to do as the captain told you and keep me company,' she said without thinking, and his deep chuckle brought a flush to her cheeks.

'I don't know—it sounds as if it has definite possibilities!' he murmured lazily, and suddenly he seemed menacing in quite another way—a way she found all too appealing.

'Don't be unprofessional,' she said a little huskily. 'Remember your hypocritic oath, Dr Bradshaw!'

He stood up suddenly, the smile wiped from his face. 'That's Hippocratic, and I'm well aware of its ramifications,' he said harshly, and turned towards the door.

Maggie was astonished. What was wrong with him? 'Ben?'

'Take it easy for a day or two, and you'll be fine. If you need any painkillers or you think it needs support, I'll be in the medical centre. Goodnight.'

Her whispered 'goodnight' bounced off the closed door. What on earth had she said? She was joking.

Was the Hippocratic oath in some way involved in
the mystery of his past?

With a groan of frustration, she eased herself
carefully off the edge of the bunk and prepared for
bed, her thoughts full of Ben and his strange and
apparently inconsistent behaviour.

What had happened to him?

And what was happening to her? She was in
danger of becoming hopelessly involved with him—
or she had been, until a thoughtless remark had sent
him running for cover. Now she had probably lost
her chance—and it was probably just as well.

With a sigh she climbed into bed and fell instantly,
dreamlessly asleep.

Maggie woke with a dull ache in her left ankle, and
for a while she considered Ben's advice to take it
easy, but with only eight days of the cruise left it
seemed too sensible for words.

Throwing back the bedclothes, she swung her legs
over the side and stood up. So far so good. Gingerly,
she tested her weight on the bad ankle. Uh-uh! Not
so smart. She sat down again.

Rats, she thought. I'll have to take it easy after
all.

Hopping carefully, she got herself ready in shorts
and T-shirt over her bikini, grabbed a little hold-all
with sunscreen, a beach-towel and a good book and
set off for the lift at a steady limp.

Emerging on to Malacca Deck, she made her way
to the Frangipani Room where she could hear the
unmistakable sound of breakfast being served.

The steward asked her her cabin number and
escorted her to a table for six with a lovely view out

over the water. She was the only person at the table, and was feeling self-conscious when Rhoda appeared at her side.

'Got any room for me? I have the distinct feeling that the people on my table are going to turn out to be the most crashing bores imaginable—and anyway, I want to ask you all sorts of searching personal questions about that lovely man!'

Maggie laughed. 'Come and join me—you can have my grandmother's seat, I'm sure. Actually I was feeling a bit lost.'

Rhoda nodded understandingly. 'Yes, it was a long time after I was widowed before I felt quite at home in a restaurant on my own. So tell me—how did you get on with him?'

Maggie fiddled with her cutlery. 'Quite well at first, but I seem to have said something that's upset him.'

'He didn't look upset last night!'

'No, it was later,' Maggie explained, and gave Rhoda an edited version.

'Oh, you poor thing! Darling, how simply *rotten* for you—is it agony?'

'Not really,' Maggie laughed. 'In fact sitting like this I can hardly feel it. It's only when I stand or walk—oh, lord, there he is!'

Rhoda swivelled her head and gave Ben the benefit of her ten-megawatt smile as he crossed the room towards them. In normal day-dress of crisp white shorts, short-sleeved open-necked white shirt and white shoes and socks, he looked even better, if possible, than he had in formal evening dress. Rhoda whistled quietly under her breath.

'Good morning, Doctor,' she purred as he drew

level with them, and Ben gave her a slightly strained smile and pulled out the chair next to Maggie.

'Good morning,' he replied, and sat down sideways on the chair, facing Maggie. 'Hi. How's the patient today?'

She smiled to ease the tension and tried not to stare. 'Not too bad. I'm going to take your advice, though.'

'Good.'

He paused, and Rhoda stood up, her brilliant smile in place. 'Will you children excuse me? I've just seen someone I want a word with—won't be a mo.'

She flitted across the room, scarf trailing colourfully, and they watched her go.

Then Maggie turned back to Ben and touched his hand. 'About last night—I'm sorry I implied you were being unprofessional. It was unforgivable.'

'You were absolutely right——'

'No, I wasn't! After all that had gone before, you were acting as a friend with medical knowledge giving first aid, rather than the ship's doctor giving a formal consultation. I was only teasing. I'm sorry you took me seriously.'

He was silent for a moment, and then he looked up with a rueful smile that didn't quite reach his eyes. 'I'm sorry, too. I'm inclined to over-react. You just hit a nerve. Anyway, I'm the ship's doctor before I'm anything else, and it wouldn't hurt to remember it. With my entertainment duties it's a fine line that's often blurred—but never more so than with you.' He sighed. 'Where are you spending the day?'

'I thought I'd find a shady spot on deck and read—
maybe swim?'

'Mind you don't burn.'

She hefted her hold-all. 'I've got some factor
twenty-five sunscreen in here.'

'You'll need it. Have a lovely day. I'll see you
later.'

He stood up, waved to Rhoda and left the room.

Rhoda excused herself and came straight back.

'Well? Did you sort out your little disagreement?'

Maggie had to smile. 'I think we may have done.
Ah, here's the steward—shall we order?'

It was a long, lazy day, and Ben drifted in and out
of it with a smile and a wave, pausing sometimes to
top up Maggie's sunscreen cream or check on the
progress of her ankle.

It made it very difficult to keep him at a distance,
because, while she hadn't wanted to leave matters
so there was bad feeling between them, on the other
hand she didn't want to encourage his attentions to
the point where he would think an affair was inevi-
table—because it wasn't.

At least she told herself that, but when he perched
on the end of her sunbed and grasped her ankle
firmly in his large, warm hands, smoothing the skin
with his thumbs while his hair-roughened thigh
brushed against her calf and his eyes sent wicked
messages to her fevered imagination, it was hard to
believe that she would have the strength to turn
away from him if he ever really tried to seduce her.

At four o'clock she went back down to her cabin
for a rest before dinner, and then dressed with extra
care, refusing to admit to herself that it had anything

to do with a certain tall, blond doctor who had insinuated himself into her life.

It was New Year's Eve, and in five hours they would be crossing the Equator. The promised party would undoubtedly be riotous and trail on until the morning, and she just hoped her ankle would stand up to it. Not that it mattered. No one would be affected if she slipped quietly away just after midnight.

Except maybe Ben.

Ignoring the sudden thudding of her heart, Maggie fastened the single tiny pearl button at the neck of the cream crêpe de Chine gown and stood back to inspect her handiwork.

Oh, dear. It's another of those dresses, she thought wearily. I really must stop taking Jo and Annie shopping with me.

There was a tap at the door, and Ben's voice curled around her senses.

'Maggie? Are you ready?'

She took a deep breath and opened the door.

He stood looking at her for endless moments, which gave her the perfect opportunity to study him in turn. And he looked gorgeous. Tall, broad, devastatingly masculine, the little-boy look banished in favour of an appraisal that was elemental in its intensity.

'My God,' he breathed, and closed his eyes, opening them again slowly. 'Turn round,' he instructed, and she noticed with rather nervous amusement that his voice was slightly rasping.

She twirled slowly, and then came to rest facing him again.

'Losing your voice?' she teased.

'Losing my grip, I think,' he replied gruffly, and with a deep sigh he offered her his arm. 'I think we need to be among people before I give in to the urge to tumble you on to your bunk and ravish you before dinner.'

Maggie laughed, but as she looked up and met his eyes she realised he was only half joking.

Thank goodness he was a gentleman!

Dinner was wonderful, each course outdoing the one before, and by the time Maggie had fought her way through the French onion soup, the lobster tails in an exquisite sauce and the beef Wellington, she was ready to give in.

Then the dessert trolley arrived, and she simply had to succumb to the crêpes with a *flambéd* dark cherry filling, drenched with thick, delicious double cream.

'My arteries will never forgive me,' she said laughingly, and Ben beside her smiled and stole a cherry dripping with cream.

'Just testing,' he murmured, and declined his own portion, choosing instead a cup of rich black coffee.

She couldn't finish, and Ben picked up her fork and speared the last few cherries. She watched, fascinated, as his lips closed on the fork and he withdrew it, a sensuous smile on his face. He licked his lips and sighed.

'I don't think I'm going to be able to move,' Maggie confided, somewhat distracted by the look in his eyes.

'You need a walk on deck. Come on. Excuse us, please, ladies and gentlemen. A little fresh air!'

They left a polite murmur behind them which

rapidly changed into idle speculation, and made their way out on to the deck.

Already passengers were beginning to drift out, and they leant on the rail and watched the flying fish leaping out of the water.

'What's the programme for this evening?' Maggie asked lazily, not at all interested in moving from her comfortable position against Ben's side.

'Dancing and cabaret until nearly midnight in the Penang Lounge, and then crossing the Equator at midnight with the captain dressed as Neptune. It's quite a laugh, I gather. Then more dancing and disco and drinking and what you will until dawn. The casino's open for those who think their luck might have changed with the advent of the New Year, and then breakfast is served for those who can tolerate it pretty much as required until midday.'

'What happens then?'

'They change the menu!'

Maggie chuckled. 'It sounds as if you'll have quite a few patients!'

He laughed. 'Inevitably. I have a large supply of hangover and indigestion remedies available for the over-indulged—talking of which, how are you feeling?'

'Over-indulged! I'll survive—it's entirely my own fault!'

He chuckled. 'How's the ankle?'

She flexed it thoughtfully. 'It seems better.'

'Better enough to dance?'

'Disco?' she asked doubtfully.

He turned towards her with a lazy smile. 'Actually, I had in mind something rather slower and more romantic. I've eaten far too much myself

to jiggle about, and anyway it seems like a good
idea.'

Maggie thought it seemed like a crazy idea, but
her wretchedly willing head nodded of its own
accord and she found herself going with him to the
Penang Lounge where couples were moving slowly
to the music.

'Too crowded,' he decided, and led her out on
deck. The sunbeds had been cleared away to make
room for the night's revelry, and apart from a few
couples similarly engaged they had the deck to
themselves.

He held out his hand. 'May I have the honour of
this dance?' he murmured, and she stepped into his
arms with a tiny sigh of resignation.

He held her lightly and very properly, until she
turned unwarily and jarred her ankle. Then he
pulled her more firmly against him and offered her
the support of his arms. 'Better?' he said softly, his
breath teasing her hair, and she nodded, sliding her
arms round his waist and leaning into him.

'Much.'

They clung together in the moonlight, swaying
gently to the soft music that washed over them under
the star-spangled tropic sky, and Maggie wondered
what on earth she was thinking about to allow herself
so close to an absolute stranger.

Except that he didn't seem like a stranger, and
after twenty-eight years her body had evidently
decided that her mind had had quite long enough
and needed a helping hand.

Perhaps it had been easy to walk away before
because she had never met anyone sufficiently
tempting? As she had told Ben, she was extremely

picky about her boyfriends—to the extent that she hadn't had one for the past two years, and the ones before that had merely been convenient escorts. Undoubtedly there had been those who had felt cheated when she refused to express her gratitude for their company in the accepted fashion, but it wasn't a fashion she had any intention of adopting for herself.

Until tonight.

Idly, she wondered whether they would end up in bed after all the revelry was over. Somehow she wouldn't be surprised.

'Time for the cabaret,' he murmured, and she dragged herself back to earth—or deck, or whatever—and allowed Ben to ease her gently away from him.

A small, unbidden whimper of distress rose in her throat, and he brushed her lips with his. 'Shh,' he whispered. 'I know. Later. Don't worry, I'm not letting you go.'

Firmly at his side, she allowed him to lead her back into the Penang Lounge for the cabaret.

Apparently it was hysterically funny, because the passengers were all clutching their sides and laughing until the tears ran down their cheeks, but Maggie had eyes and ears only for Ben, and when he turned and winked at her she knew he was feeling the same way.

When the cabaret was over they made their way out on deck again, gathering round the pool, and shortly before midnight their portly captain appeared, scantily clad in a few strands of strategically placed artificial seaweed, brandishing a trident and singing sea-shanties with great gusto and only slightly off-key.

At the stroke of twelve his trident was removed and he was thrown into the pool, amid great cheers, and emerged dripping and smiling broadly to kiss all the women passengers.

And he wasn't the only one in demand. As he reached Maggie and clutched her arms with slightly damp hands before bestowing a smacking kiss on her cheek, she saw a tarty blonde with legs that went on forever and arms like an octopus envelope Ben and press her lips firmly to his in an unmistakable invitation.

'Happy New Year,' she crooned, and seized him again.

Maggie turned away and allowed herself to be kissed by variously over-enthusiastic male passengers until she felt a hand on her arm and shook it off, heartily sick of the whole business.

Damn it, she was jealous! Serious stuff, being in lust, she confessed disgustedly to herself, and felt the hand return to her arm, shackling her wrist in strong fingers.

She turned to quell the enthusiastic Lothario and found herself looking into Ben's furious eyes.

'Did you have to let them *all* kiss you?'

'Huh!' She was enraged. 'Me? What about you and that—that——?'

'Barbie-doll?' he offered, and she suddenly saw the funny side. A bubble of laughter rose in her throat, and Ben's lips twitched.

'Come on, let's get out of here.'

He led her round the corner, up the ladder and through the little gate that led to their very own private sanctuary, and there he drew her into his arms.

'Happy New Year,' he murmured against her lips, and then he was kissing her with all the pent-up feeling of the last few hours, holding her as she had wanted him to hold her since she had opened her cabin door to him at seven o'clock.

She sagged against him, her legs unable to support her, and he groaned low in his throat and turned her so that she was propped up against a bulkhead, then his hands dropped to her waist and slid slowly upwards.

Because of the cut of the dress she had been unable to wear a bra, and she had a moment's pang that he would be disappointed in the small size of her breasts, but, as his hands cupped them, his breath hissed out between his teeth and she felt a deep shudder run through him.

'I want to look at you,' he whispered, and deftly dispatched the single pearl button that held the back of the neck. The gown was slashed from nape to waist, and as he eased it over her shoulders the bodice fell softly to her hips and left her open to his gaze.

His face was in shadow, but the moonlight gleamed brightly on her pale skin, leaving nothing to the imagination. She moved to cover herself, but he caught her hands, trapping them as he stared at her hungrily.

'You're perfect,' he rasped, 'a moonlit goddess. Maggie, I want you. Now. Tonight.'

Her throat was dry from need, and the only word she could manage was his name. It was enough.

Tugging the shoulders roughly back into place, his trembling fingers refastened the button.

'Come on,' he said gruffly. 'Let's go somewhere where we won't be disturbed.'

Mindlessly she followed him, her defences in tatters. Her legs were trembling so badly that they were almost out of control, and if they had been alone in the lift she had the distinct feeling it would have been all over there and then.

But they weren't alone, and somehow managed to survive the endless descent without reaching for each other.

He was inserting the key in her cabin door when a steward called him and came hurrying towards them.

'Dr Ben, excuse me, there is a man urgently needing your attention.'

Ben groaned quietly under his breath.

'OK, Ah Seng, thank you. I'll be with you in a moment.'

He pushed open the door, followed Maggie in and folded her against his chest with a ragged sigh.

'I'm sorry,' he muttered. his voice rich with frustration and apology. 'Duty calls. I won't be long. Wait for me.'

With a brief kiss, he was gone.

CHAPTER THREE

MAGGIE waited, as instructed, and as the minutes ticked by and turned into hours so her heart slowed and common sense returned.

Whatever was she thinking about? He was an inveterate flirt, a rootless, itinerant playboy with some nameless hang-up about his past—no, she was better off without him.

Ignoring the tug of disappointment in the region of her heart, she hung up her dress, climbed into bed and then got up again to lock her door.

In fact she needn't have bothered, because Ben didn't come back that night and she didn't see him again at all the following day, although she did see the Barbie-doll from the poolside leaving the medical centre still dressed—if you could call it that—in the scrap of tinsel she had been draped in the night before.

By dinner that night he still hadn't appeared, and, feeling rather miffed, she squandered some of her grandmother's more-than-generous spending money in the casino.

So he had thought better of it—well, so had she. He was obviously not worth wasting her energy on—especially not if he was prepared to settle for that ghastly tart! She was going to make a New Year's resolution to avoid him for the remainder of the cruise. It shouldn't be difficult.

Her ankle was much better, and she decided to

take a stroll on deck. It was too crowded for her
taste, and, slipping quietly away, she took the route
she had followed with Ben and went through the
gate marked 'Authorised Personnel Only'.

Perhaps it was instinct that led her to him, but she
was unsurprised to find him standing there alone in
the moonlight, his arms propped on the teak rail,
staring out over the night sea. So much for her
resolution!

'You didn't come back,' she said accusingly before
she could stop herself.

He straightened and turned towards her, and she
was shocked to see how tired he looked.

'Maggie,' he murmured absently, and, lifting a
hand, he caught the stray lock of hair blowing across
her face and tucked it behind her ear.

'I thought you'd fallen overboard,' she said
brightly, trying to make light of the wild tumult his
touch had caused.

'I'm sorry about last night, I've been rather busy.
I've got a bit of a virus on my hands—some kind of
mysterious flu bug. That on top of the rush for
antacids and aspirin!'

And spending time with the Barbie-doll, she
thought uncharitably, but her better nature defeated
the little spurt of jealousy. 'Have you got any help—
a nurse, perhaps?'

He gave a tiny spurt of laughter. 'She's off sick—
malaria. My steward's with the patients now, but I
just felt I had to get some fresh air.'

Maggie's hand came up and caressed his cheek all
on its own. 'You look exhausted, Ben. Did you sleep
at all last night?'

He shook his head. 'Not much. I was going to

come and explain, but—to be honest, until we know what this is, I was keeping out of everybody's way. Rodrigues is in touch with head office—we may end up quarantined until it's identified.'

She forgot the tinsel-wrapped octopus. Perhaps he was telling the truth? 'What are the symptoms?'

'Oh, dozens—tiredness, headaches, muscle aches and pains, rapidly rising fever, dry cough. The worst have nausea and abdominal pain, and breathlessness.'

'Sounds like rather nasty flu.'

'It does, doesn't it?'

Maggie hesitated for a moment. 'Ben, if you need a hand—I'm a doctor.'

He gave a short laugh. 'You're kidding?'

'No, I'm not kidding. I was trying to keep it quiet because—well, you know what it's like.'

'Oh, yes.' He sighed. 'God, Maggie, are you real? I can barely cope at the moment with four patients, but if we get many more we'll be running at full stretch. The odd hour of cover would be wonderful.'

'I wasn't offering you the odd hour, Ben. I was offering to share it.'

He stared at her in silence for a moment.

'Maggie, I couldn't——'

'Why not—for the patients?'

'Why not? You're on holiday!'

She shrugged. 'If I'm needed, that comes first.'

His eyes scanned her face for a moment longer, then he let out his breath in a rush. 'OK. You'll probably live to regret it, but for the sake of my patients I have to say yes. Thank you.'

He pulled her into his arms and hugged her gently. 'Is your ankle up to it?'

'I'll cope.'

'Good. I can always put it in a cast.'

'I'll be able to kick you then.'

'I'll risk it.'

She chuckled. 'You must be desperate.'

'I am. Come on, I can't leave Ah Seng down there alone forever.'

Together they made their way back to Java Deck and then parted, Ben to the medical centre, Maggie to her cabin to change out of her fine feathers into something more businesslike.

When she arrived at the door of the medical centre, she was greeted by Ben's harassed Chinese steward, whose relief was almost tangible.

'Ah Seng, this is Dr Wells, who's going to help us,' Ben told him, and he smiled beamingly at her.

'Marvellous news,' he said with a grin. 'Dr Ben plenty busy tonight—another new patient.'

'I think he's recruiting them when my back's turned,' Ben said drily.

It was a hectic night. Maggie discovered nursing skills she didn't know she had, and during the night she took turns with Ben to monitor the patients who were ill enough to be admitted to the medical centre, with visits when necessary to the others. By morning all but one of the five patients were in the little hospital, and the worst affected patient, Vic Matthews, a man in his early sixties who was a heavy smoker, was confused and dehydrated.

Ben set up an IV line and ran in some normal saline to boost his fluids, and then, leaving Maggie in charge, he went to confer with Captain Rodrigues.

Maggie spent the time he was gone trying to get some kind of history from the patients—and, more particularly, some kind of link. She took their cabin numbers, found out where they'd eaten and what they'd eaten, and could find nothing to link them at all.

When Ben came back they went into the dispensary and shut the door. 'We're making a detour to Jakarta. The old boy's going to be air-lifted back to Singapore. I have a nasty feeling he isn't going to make it, and I don't want him dying on my ship. The others don't seem too bad.'

Maggie wasn't so sure. 'Look—can you find a link? I don't know what connection there could be between them—can you see anything I've missed?'

Ben studied the data, located the cabins on a map and shook his head.

'I'll check with the ship's engineer to find out if they have a common hot water supply or anything else, but it doesn't look like it—which blows my theory out of the window.'

Maggie cocked her head on one side and raised an eyebrow. 'Theory?' she asked.

'Yes—legionnaires' disease.'

She snapped her fingers. 'Of course—have you got any erythromycin on board?'

'Maggie, it can't be that—there's no link.'

'There must be. We just haven't found it. In the meantime we ought to try—it can't hurt. Have you got any?'

'Yes, of course—enough to start them off, and we can pick up more in Jakarta. We'll be there in four hours. Until this virus or bacillus is positively identified, we're quarantined, by the way. The passengers are going to love it.'

Maggie laughed tiredly. 'They shouldn't complain. At least the rest of them get to sleep.'

Ben's forehead creased with concern. 'Maggie, I'm sorry. How's your ankle bearing up?'

She shrugged. 'Bit tender, but I'll live. I wish we could find the missing link. I'll keep talking to them—perhaps something will come up.'

'It must be a water link—I wonder if they've all used the pool?'

'I'll check. How about some coffee?' she suggested.

But the pool idea drew a blank. Only two of the patients had even been near it.

She was just checking Mr Matthews's IV line and oxygen supply when he gave a ragged gasp and collapsed.

'Ben!' she yelled, and, picking up his wrist, she felt fruitlessly for a pulse. Ben appeared at her side, his brow drawn into a frown.

'What's wrong?'

'He's arrested. Help me resuscitate him.'

She pulled back the bedclothes and crossed her hands over his sternum, pressing rhythmically to massage his heart and circulate the blood. After a few seconds she realised that Ben was standing motionless beside her, frozen.

'For God's sake, do something!' she hissed, but Ben continued to stand there, an anguished expression on his face.

'Ben?'

She reached out her hand and touched him, and he started slightly, his eyes shocked as they met hers.

'Help me,' she pleaded softly.

He took a deep, steadying breath and then snapped into action, taking over the cardiac massage and instructing her to set up an airway and inject atropine and adrenalin into the giving set.

Ah Seng materialised out of nowhere and together they unclipped the bed from its mounting and moved it through into the tiny operating theatre.

Once there they connected Mr Matthews up to the cardiac monitor and watched in relief as his heart picked up a rather distorted rhythm.

'He's fibrillating. Let's give him a belt,' Ben said calmly, and Maggie and Ah Seng stood back as he applied the paddles of the defibrillator to Vic Matthews's massive, fleshy chest.

The man arched and flopped, and the trace blipped and steadied.

'Good, he's back in sinus—after a fashion. Well done, Maggie. Thank you, Ah Seng. Maggie, perhaps you could go and reassure the other patients while I just check he's settling? They're probably a little distressed.'

'Sure.'

Walking back out into the main ward with a smile, she announced, 'He's OK. His heart had a little hiccup, but it's fine again now. I'm sorry we frightened you all.'

There was a murmur of relief from all the patients, and Maggie pulled up a chair next to Mrs Davis, whose condition was giving her cause for concern.

'OK?' she asked quietly.

'I am—but what about him?' She indicated the closed door of the operating theatre. 'Is he going to get better?' she asked quietly.

'I hope so,' Maggie told her. 'Certainly his heart's

giving him trouble, but there's no reason why it shouldn't settle down once the treatment improves his general condition. Now we think we've identified the germ we can tackle it more effectively, so he stands more chance.'

'He's got a dreadful cough, too,' Mrs Davis said with a shake of her head. 'I noticed in the hotel one night that he was having trouble breathing——'

'Hotel? What hotel?'

Mrs Davis blinked at her. 'Oh, well, we had a stopover—four days in Singapore. Lovely hotel—I'm sorry, I can't seem to remember the name.'

'Mrs Davis, can you remember if everybody here was on the same stopover?'

The woman lifted her head and shoulders up and peered along the row of beds, then she fell back with a sigh.

'Now you come to mention it, dear, I believe they were.'

'Thanks.' Maggie smiled and squeezed her hand, and hurried back into the operating theatre just as Ben was coming out.

'What's wrong now?' he asked worriedly.

'Nothing—Ben, I think I've got your link!'

While Maggie set up the intravenous lines to deliver the erythromycin in the most effective way possible, Ben tracked down the captain and the purser. The affected patients had, indeed, all been on the same stopover, and when they checked with the hotel they discovered that an outbreak of a mystery virus was being investigated. However, *legionella* was still not confirmed, and until it was the ship had to remain quarantined.

The other passengers who had been on the stop-over were quicky traced, called together and examined, and given details of symptoms which they might expect. Ben emphasised that if it was indeed legionnaires', although it was an infection, it was not contagious, and so they couldn't spread the disease by contact with the other passengers. However, until that was confirmed they would be isolated. The cabins on Java Deck were cleared, the passengers relocated and their condition would continue to be monitored.

Although none of them was obviously ill yet, one passenger, a man in his early sixties with a persistent bronchitis, gave Ben some cause for concern, and he and several of the others were started on erythromycin prophylactically just to be on the safe side.

By the time they had all been examined, dosed, reassured and settled into their new quarters, the ship had arrived in Jakarta and they were able to off-load Mr Matthews to a waiting air-ambulance.

Ben and Maggie watched him go from the deck, his wife accompanying him.

'She looks worried to death,' Maggie commented, and Ben shook his head.

'What d'you reckon?' Maggie asked quietly.

'He's a high-risk patient. There's too much stacked against him—if he didn't smoke sixty a day it might be different. No, Maggie, he doesn't stand a snowflake's chance in hell of pulling through.'

'Is that why you were reluctant to resuscitate him?'

Ben met her eyes, his own filled with pain. 'Maybe,' he replied eventually, but he obviously didn't want to discuss it any further, and Maggie didn't feel she could press.

They turned back to the medical centre and the patients for whom their presence held some hope.

The captain called all the other passengers together, and Ben explained to them the seriousness of the situation for the sick passengers still remaining on the vessel. He did his best to reassure them that he was confident of the diagnosis, but until confirmation was received the other stopover passengers had been isolated as a precautionary measure.

Needless to say, they didn't like it, and a predictable number kicked up a fuss and demanded their money back.

'Will the cruise line pay up?' Maggie asked him later that evening.

'Oh, undoubtedly. They'll probably offer them either a refund or another cruise of their choice.'

'Well, that seems fair,' she said.

They were in the dispensary stacking the new supplies of erythromycin and rifampicin which they had picked up in Jakarta.

Ben seemed deep in thought, and when Ah Seng brought them in a cup of coffee he sat staring blankly into space and stirring the cup relentlessly.

'You'll wear a hole in it,' Maggie commented mildly, and he sighed and gave a weary little chuckle.

'Sorry. I was just thinking about Vic Matthews.'

'Is there any news?'

He nodded. 'He arrested twice in the air-ambulance, but they got him to the Singapore General still alive, although only just. It's up to them now.'

'Do you want to talk about it?'

Ben looked at her, his eyes curiously intense. 'I'd rather talk about us.'

Maggie looked away, confused by the sudden change of tack. 'What about us?' she asked, a trifle breathlessly.

His fingers reached out and brushed her cheek. 'There's the little matter of last night,' he murmured.

'Last night?' she whispered, definitely breathless now as his fingers trailed down her jaw and teased the soft skin beneath her ear. 'Nothing happened last night.'

'No—unfortunately. But I can wait—if I have to. I want to be able to give you my undivided attention.' His fingers slid under the neckline of her T-shirt and dipped low over her breasts, his knuckles grazing the soft skin and bringing an involuntary moan to her lips. 'At the moment that isn't possible, but after we dock at Singapore and hand over our sick passengers to the SGH that will change. Then,' he murmured huskily, his fingers trapping her chin and tilting it towards him, 'I promise you my full and undivided attention for the remainder of the cruise.'

And what about afterwards? she wanted to scream. When you've given me your full and undivided attention long enough to get me into bed, what then? Nothing, that's what. Just however many thousand miles of ocean and mountains and deserts between us.

She stood up. 'I think I'll get an early night. Wake me at three; I'll take over.'

'You won't escape, Maggie,' he said softly, his voice following her to the door. 'You can run away from me, but you can't run away from yourself. It'll happen, as surely as the sun will rise at six tomorrow morning.'

'You're very confident,' she replied with a somewhat shaky laugh.

'You'll be awake, not me. See for yourself.'

He woke her at three, as she had requested, with a brief bulletin of the condition of their patients and a cup of tea.

She showered quickly, pulled on fresh clothes and made her way to the medical centre. Ben was in the dispensary writing up notes.

'Mrs Davis is looking worse, so I've started her on rifampicin as well, to boost the action of the erythromycin. Otherwise they seem stable.'

'Good. Any chance of another cup of tea?' she asked, eyeing the pot at his elbow longingly.

'Yes—help yourself. I just want to get this written up and I'm off to bed.'

She filled her cup, then set the pot down again beside him. His head was bowed over the notes, and she could see the strong cords of muscle in the back of his neck beneath the neatly trimmed hair. It looked soft and thick, and she had to clench her fists to stop her fingers from burying themselves in the enticing mass.

With a weary sigh he straightened and tipped back his head, grinning at her tiredly. 'All yours, Dr Wells,' he said a little huskily. 'Enjoy the dawn. I'll see you later.'

Enjoy the dawn.

She glanced through the porthole in the end wall of the little ward, and saw nothing but blackness. Her eyes were gritty, her senses dulled with tiredness and yet alert by habit and instinct. Dawn seemed a long way away—and so did romance.

Mrs Davis was very breathless and uncomfortable, and Maggie did what she could to settle her. At four-thirty, she was called to the cabin of the bronchitic man about whom Ben had expressed concern. Sure enough, he was showing definite signs of having contracted the disease, and Maggie called two stewards to transfer him to the medical centre so that she could keep an eye on him better.

All six beds were now occupied, and Maggie just hoped that no one else developed any symptoms before their arrival at Singapore.

Shortly before six the phone in the dispensary rang quietly. It was the captain, to say that the outbreak in the hotel had been confirmed as legionnaires' disease, and that quarantine restrictions had been lifted.

There was also the sad but not unexpected news that Vic Matthews's heart had failed yet again, this time for good.

Thanking Captain Rodrigues for the update, Maggie went back out into the quiet ward and glanced round. All the patients seemed to be sleeping peacefully, and Mr Grey, the bronchitic, was more comfortable now on oxygen.

She stood by the porthole and watched as a line appeared between the sea and sky. In a matter of minutes the sky lightened and the edge of the sun crawled over the horizon, flooding the world with pink and gold.

'Incredible, isn't it?' a voice said softly behind her.

Maggie glanced at her watch. Six exactly.

'What are you doing up? You should still be asleep.'

'I wanted to watch the dawn with you. It happened, you see, just as I promised.'

Her heart thudded at his words. Was her life as predetermined as the dawn?

'How are things?'

Things? Confused. Maggie turned away from the window and drew a sharp breath as her eyes took in his appearance. He was wearing a short navy towelling robe that hung open in a deep V over his chest, and she could see the drops of moisture on his skin beneath the light scatter of hair.

He had showered but not shaved, and the roughness of his jaw beneath the laughing eyes gave him a slightly rakish look.

'What's with the designer stubble?' she asked quietly, leading him to the dispensary.

He ran his hand over his jaw and the rasp of stubble on skin skittered over her nerve-endings, leaving her tremblingly alive.

He closed the door softly and pulled her into his arms.

'Good morning,' he murmured, and his lips came down and settled gently against her startled mouth.

'Ben, no,' she protested feebly, but his lips stole her words and all her resolutions, leaving her weak and helpless in his arms.

'You taste so good,' he mumbled, his lips nuzzling the soft skin beneath her ear. Her hands released their death-grip on the lapels of his towelling robe and slid unasked on to his skin, testing the texture with eager fingers.

The combination of satin skin, soft, springy hair

and the dew left by the shower was intoxicating. Before her eyes a droplet gathered strength and slithered slowly down his chest, and her tongue came out and captured it before it could escape.

Beneath her hands his chest shuddered as he let out an unsteady groan.

'God, Maggie, if you don't want me to take you right here on the edge of the desk, just yards from our patients, you'd better stop that,' he said raggedly.

Suddenly aware again of her surroundings and the inadvisability of her actions, she dropped her hands and spun away, struggling to control her breathing.

'You started it,' she accused childishly.

'And I'll willingly finish it, but, though it grieves me to say so, here and now isn't the time.' He filled the kettle and plugged it in. 'What was the phone call?'

'Oh—the captain. They've confirmed that the outbreak in the hotel was caused by the *legionella* bacillus, and so the quarantine restrictions have been lifted.'

'Good. It's nice to be right.'

'Mmm. Yes, well, there's something else you were right about. Vic Matthews didn't make it.'

He sighed heavily. 'Damn. It would have been nice to be wrong about that. How about the others? I see we've acquired another patient.'

'Yes, Mr Grey. He's on oxygen, and I've started him on rifampicin as well. I don't think we can afford to mess about with him, and we don't want another casualty.'

'No.' Ben sighed again and spooned coffee into

two mugs. 'Frankly, the sooner we get to Singapore
the happier I'll be—for several reasons!'

He looked up and caught her eye, and gave a
roguish, little-boy grin. Maggie blushed and looked
away.

Somehow she had the feeling that if she didn't get
off the ship at Singapore and stay off it she was going
to end up precisely as Ben predicted, and loving
every second of it. That wasn't the problem.

More of a problem was how she'd feel afterwards,
because she wasn't so naïve that she didn't realise
the effect making love with Ben would have on her
feelings.

Now, she found him fascinating—funny, enter-
taining, capable of great tenderness and compassion,
sometimes moody, touched in some indefinable way
by the mystery of his past. Already she yearned to
know him better, to have her questions answered.
For days her body had raged out of control, but now
her mind was joining in, and she realised that she
was within a hair's breadth of falling in love.

Which would be fine back in the homely security
of the Audley Memorial, but here, on the other side
of the world and as far removed from reality as it
was possible to get, it would be nothing but the
height of folly.

CHAPTER FOUR

FOLLY or not, Maggie was defenceless against Ben's straightforward and unaffected charm.

She tried to avoid him, but somehow fate—or was it actually Ben?—conspired against her and she found herself rpeatedly brushing up against him—literally.

On one occasion she turned round in the dispensary to find Ben's body blocking her way, and the subtle movement of the ship swayed him gently against her.

He deepened the pressure with an intimacy that brought the colour to her cheeks and a soft gasp to her lips.

'I never knew medicine was a contact sport,' she managed breathlessly, and he grinned and let her go.

'You learn something new every day,' he told her laughingly, and left her alone until the next time.

By mid-morning she was not only irritated, she was aching with frustration, a frustration that boiled over when he cornered her in the sluice and trailed hot kisses over the nape of her neck beneath her hair.

'Oh, God, Ben, please stop,' she pleaded, and to her utter humiliation, she felt tears start to trickle down her cheeks.

'I don't want to stop,' he murmured against her skin, and then stiffened when he heard a little sob

61

break free. 'Maggie? Ah, love, don't cry. I'm sorry, I didn't mean to upset you. Do you want me to leave you alone?'

'Yes—no—I don't know!' she hiccuped, and he turned her into his chest and hugged her until she sniffed to a halt. Then he produced a clean hanky and mopped her face, told her to blow, and then ordered her to go to bed and rest for a while.

'What about you?' she asked miserably.

'What about me? I've been free-wheeling for months. You're at the end of your tether. Go on, I can cope for a few hours on my own. I'll bring you a late lunch. Go on, get to bed. I'll see you later.'

'Call me if you need me,' she said unwisely, and then, blushing furiously at his wry chuckle, she fled to the sanctity of her cabin, to lie restlessly on the bunk for nearly an hour before falling into a fitful sleep.

She woke to find Ben setting down a tray of fresh and tempting salad on the table between the two bunks.

'Lunch,' he told her with a strained smile, and Maggie blinked to clear the fog from her mind and tried to smile back.

'Thank you.'

'Don't thank me, Ah Seng brought it down. Take your time, and go back to sleep again if you want afterwards. It's fairly quiet at the moment. Or you could go up on deck and have a swim and lie in the sun if you like now the isolation isn't necessary.'

'Oh—right.' She struggled to sit up, tugging the bedclothes up with her to cover her top. Without thinking she had slipped off her clothes and got into bed in her bra and pants, and now, of course. . .

'What about you—aren't you staying for lunch?' she asked—somewhat inanely, as there was clearly only the one plate.

He gave a short, humourless laugh. 'I've already eaten,' he told her. 'But in any case, I don't think I should stay, do you? I might be tempted to do something we'll both regret.'

His eyes strayed over her shoulders, and he reached out a hand to stroke the smooth skin.

'Mind you don't burn if you go up on deck,' he cautioned, his voice professional, while his hand trailed over her shoulder and down her arm in a tender caress that was anything but.

'I won't burn,' she assured him, her voice somewhat husky. 'I'll use sunscreen.'

'You mind you do,' he murmured, his eyes fixed on his fingertip as it wandered back up the inside of her arm and beneath the hem of the sheet, brushing tauntingly against the soft swell of her breasts.

Then he turned and walked away, leaving Maggie almost helpless with longing and wondering why no one had ever invented a lovescreen to protect delicate maidens from the dangerous rays given off by men.

After she had eaten her lunch, she showered and dressed and from an ingrained sense of duty went back to the medical centre, to find that two more of the passengers from the same tour had succumbed to the disease during the course of the day.

Ben was looking harassed and far too busy to give her any trouble, she thought, but during the course of the afternoon and evening she found her eyes straying to him over and over again, and she realised that his very presence was enough to give her trouble, both physical and emotional.

Physical she could deal with, denial of her body's responses being second nature after all these years. What was much harder was the pull on her emotions, and watching him as he tended to his patients with gentle humour and compassion just increased the danger to her heart.

In the end in desperation, and because he looked exhausted, she sent him to lie down and rest for a while when things settled down at about seven. It was her intention, if all went well, to leave him until about three in the morning and then go to bed herself, but the road to hell—and back, frankly— could be paved with the good intentions she had had since starting this cruise. And anyway, her reason for waking him when she did was genuine.

Mrs Davis was having trouble with her intravenous line, and Maggie felt Ben ought to have a look at it.

She knocked on his cabin door and went in, closing it softly behind her. 'Ben?'

The room was in darkness, only the quiet sound of his breathing audible over the steady hum of the engines. A bright shaft of moonlight lay on the floor, and after a few moments her eyes grew accustomed to the gloom and she was able to make out his figure spread-eagled on the bunk.

It took another couple of seconds to realise that he was naked, by which time the quality of his breathing had changed.

She glanced up at his face, thankful that he couldn't see the blush that had run over her cheeks, and found he was watching her.

'Problems?' he asked gruffly, his voice sleep-roughened.

'Yes—Mrs Davis. Her drip needs resiting, I think, but the other arm's no great shakes. I think you ought to have a look.'

'Fine.' He swung his legs over the edge of the bunk and sat up, flicking on the reading light at the head of the bunk.

It shone obliquely on his body, casting deep shadows and gliding smooth planes, highlighting the ripple of his muscles as he locked his hands togther above his head and stretched. He looked like a big, lazy golden cat, and Maggie was mesmerised.

'What's the time?' he asked on a yawn.

His obvious exhaustion brought her maternal instinct to the fore, supplanting the latent sensuality that Ben had brought so skilfully to life.

'Ten-thirty—are you all right?'

'Yes, I'm fine—why, were you offering me some of your very own special TLC?' he teased gently, and suddenly she was overwhelmingly conscious of his nakedness again.

Dear God, she thought, perhaps there is no war between maternal instinct and the urge to mate. Perhaps they're interlinked when a woman loves a man—and that was a train of thought she had no intention of following up.

'Of course not! I—I'll see you back in the ward,' she mumbled, and fled, pursued by the soft sound of his mocking laughter.

He joined her a few moments later in the ward, now repectable in white shorts and shirt, and examined Mrs Davis's arm gently. 'Yes, it's all a bit swollen, isn't it?' he agreed. 'We'll have to resite the drip. It won't take long.'

He smiled reassuringly at Mrs Davis, and led Maggie to the dispensary.

'What's wrong?' he asked when the door was shut. 'You look worried.'

'The other arm's not marvellous,' Maggie told him quietly. 'Rather you than me, put it like that.'

'Oh, great!' he said with a sigh, and found the necessary equipment to set up the drip again. 'Let's see if I can justify your faith in me.'

He could, with consummate ease, it seemed. Within a very few minutes Mrs Davis had a new drip in her arm and Ben was putting the kettle on for a cup of coffee.

'Shut the door and talk to me,' he told Maggie.

'What about?'

He shrugged. 'Anything. It just occurred to me that it's four days since we met and I know practically nothing about you. The only thing I do know is that whenever I come near you you want to go screaming home to Mother.'

She snorted. 'Hardly. I haven't been able to go screaming home to Mother for nearly twenty years.'

'Oh, God, I'm sorry. How old were you when she died?'

Maggie sighed and dropped wearily into the only chair. 'I wasn't—I mean, she didn't. Die, that is. She walked out on me and my brother—left us with my father. She ran off with her boyfriend. Heaven knows where she is now; she never bothered to keep in touch.'

'I'm sorry.'

Ben's voice was sincere, but it couldn't stop the bitterness in Maggie.

'Don't be,' she advised him harshly. 'It's all water under the bridge. I went to a very nice girls' boarding-school in Bournemouth, and learned to survive. From there I went to university, and medical college, and once I've done my registration year I'll start working for my FRCP—the perennial student, so to speak.' She laughed with false brightness, but Ben remained serious, watching her with compassionate eyes.

'So,' she said, looking awkwardly away. 'What about you?'

'Me?' He settled one hip against the counter top and cradled his coffee mug in both hands. 'I was born in London. My mother was a teacher. She died when I was twenty-five, just after I qualified. She was a wonderful woman, and I still miss her. I never really knew my father, but my mother married again when I was nine, and my stepfather has been all I could have asked and more. He's still a very important person in my life.'

'What does he think of you dashing off to the other side of the world and licking your wounds?'

Ben laughed without humour. 'Is that what you think I'm doing?'

'Isn't it?'

Maggie met his glare steadily, and after a moment he gave a slight shrug. 'Perhaps I was. Now I'm just fulfilling my obligations. As for what he thinks of it, he's very understanding, and wonderful to talk to. He's been a great help through all this—mess.'

'Mess?'

Ben straightened up and turned away.

'There was a—court case. I was cleared. It was nothing, really.'

'But it hurt.'

'Yes.'

Maggie watched his rigid shoulders as he stood with his back to her, straightening the rows of medical supplies needlessly.

'You don't want to talk about it, do you?' she asked gently.

'Not really.'

She stood up and put down her mug. 'That's fine. You'll tell me when you want to. Why don't you go back to bed?'

He kept his back to her. 'No, you go. I'll be fine. I'll wake you at four or so, OK?'

'If you're sure?'

'I'm sure. Goodnight.'

He didn't turn round or soften his dismissal with a smile, and Maggie left him, still fiddling with the dressings, a figure very much alone.

She woke to the awareness of his presence in her cabin, and blinked sleepily to clear her blurred vision.

'Ben?'

'Hi. I'm sorry to wake you, but I could do with some shut-eye, and Mr Grey isn't too good. I've put him on the ventilator—I just hope we get to Singapore in time.'

Maggie struggled to a sitting position and looked at Ben sitting on the other bunk, his elbows on his knees, his head hanging down. As she watched him he lifted his head and smiled tiredly at her.

'Did you sleep all right?'

She laughed. 'Are you kidding? After eighteen

months as a house doctor? I can sleep standing on my head!'

He chuckled. 'I know the feeling. So, are you doing your SHO year?'

She nodded. 'Yes, in Paediatrics.'

He whistled softly. 'Wow. I could never do that. It breaks me up when children die.'

'They don't always,' she reminded him. 'Sometimes we save them, and the vast majority of our work is fairly trivial in the life and death stakes.' She paused for a moment, and then asked him, 'What were you doing before—when everything went wrong?'

There was a long silence, and at first she didn't think he'd answer her. Then he spoke, and she was shocked at the hurt and disillusionment in his voice.

'I was in Accident and Emergency—the end of my second year as a registrar. I resuscitated someone who expressed his gratitude by suing me for my efforts.'

'What? Why ever should he do that?'

'Oh, it's a long story, and there isn't time. Maybe I'll tell you one day. When we've got our patients safely tucked up in hospital and I can relax, perhaps then. In the meantime,' he levered himself off the edge of the bunk and perched beside her, 'I ought to get some sleep and you ought to go and keep an eye on our sickly friends. But first. . .'

His hands cupped her shoulders lightly and he eased her up against his chest, his head close to hers.

'Ben?' she whispered.

'Good morning,' he whispered back, and his head closed the tiny space between them, his lips settling naturally against her mouth as if they belonged there.

With a tiny sigh Maggie relaxed against his hard, well-muscled body, her arms slipping round his waist as her hands flattened themselves against his spine.

It was a gentle kiss, devoid of passion, and after a moment he lifted his head and rested his cheek against her hair.

'You're a lovely girl, Maggie,' he murmured. 'I wish. . .'

She waited, but he didn't continue, and after a moment his body grew heavy in her arms.

Good grief, she thought in amazement, he's asleep!

With a chuckle of self-derision, she eased out from under his arms and wriggled out of the bunk, allowing him to topple to the pillow. Then she lifted his legs and swung them round on to the mattress, dropped a kiss on his brow and pulled on her clothes.

She would shower later, so as not to disturb him, although looking at him it would take a bomb under him to make much impact.

When she was ready she slipped out of her cabin and went along to the medical centre. Mr Grey was stable at the bottom end of seriously ill, and, after quickly checking the others, Maggie sat herself in the chair beside his bed and picked up the medical journal that Ben had obviously been reading.

It was open to a page on ethical decisions about terminally ill patients, and she read it with interest. Although the paper was by and large about adults at the end of their lives, many of the issues were relevant to paediatrics, especially neonatal care.

Judging the quality of life for another person was

impossible. All one could hope to do was maintain that quality as far as possible. Of course with an adult it was easier, in that a decision could be made jointly on whether to discontinue treatment, but how did one ask a tiny baby, brain-damaged by birth or prematurity, or cursed with a genetic disorder or physical deformity, whether the quality of his or her life would be sufficiently good to justify the pain and misery of endless treatment to sustain that life? Where did you draw the line?

Maggie put the journal down. In many ways, she thought, things were easier before the advent of modern medicine. There were no decisions about when to discontinue treatment, because there was no treatment. People were undoubtedly better off these days as far as the run-of-the-mill illnesses were concerned, but Maggie wondered if perhaps in the drive to preserve life at all cost the world had forgotten how to allow people to die with dignity.

She wondered about the background to Ben's story, the history of the man who had sued him for saving his life. Perhaps that was why Ben had been reading that article?

She stood up and walked quietly down the ward, checking the sleeping patients.

Mrs Davis, she saw, was awake and looking a little brighter. Maggie glanced at her watch. It was almost six.

'Let me do your temperature and blood-pressure, and I'll get you a nice cup of tea,' she said with a smile.

'Oh, that would be lovely. I really fancy a cup of tea this morning.'

'I think you're getting a little better, aren't you?'

Mrs Davis nodded. 'All except for this cough—I seem much chestier now.'

'You will,' Maggie assured her, 'but that'll pass. You'll feel pretty weak for some time, and it may be a couple of months before you feel your old self again, but plenty of rest should do the trick. Your temperature's down a little today—that's probably why you feel better.'

She checked the rest of her obs, filled in the chart and went into the dispensary to make a cup of tea. While the kettle boiled she checked the other patients, doing their observations without waking them, and by the time Ah Seng arrived she had made the tea for Mrs Davis, had a cup herself and started the drugs.

'You won't know how to spend time when patients go,' he said with a laugh.

'Don't worry, Ah Seng,' she told him, 'I'll find plenty to do. Lying in the sun, swimming, reading— sleeping would make a change!'

Ah Seng smiled knowingly. 'Dr Ben sleep better in your cabin, Dr Wells?'

She blushed fire-engine red. 'He came to wake me, and fell asleep,' she explained, furious with herself for feeling the need to justify Ben's presence in her cabin. 'He's very tired.'

Ah Seng smiled again, but this time with great affection. 'Dr Ben not tired now. When he first come, he very tired, not sleeping, walking all night. Now he better—OK, tired a bit today, but soon fine. Not like before. Before I worry about him. Not now. You like breakfast, Dr Wells?'

'Yes, please, Ah Seng. Just toast.'

'Toast!' he spat. 'You have proper breakfast, Dr

Wells, or you get sick like Dr Ben, and then what
good you be to him?'

Maggie surrendered. 'OK, Ah Seng. Some fruit
as well, perhaps?'

'Fruit, toast—silly woman,' he muttered as he left
the room.

Maggie smiled. He might be bossy, but Ah Seng
had been a tower of strength during the past few
days. He had changed sheets, plumped pillows,
fetched bedpans and sick-bowls, swabbed the floor
endlessly, brought food for Maggie and Ben as well
as whichever patients were able to eat, and generally
gone about his tasks with good humour and unflag-
ging energy.

He was obviously devoted to Ben, and would do
anything for him—even to the point of feeding up
his mistress, as Ah Seng evidently thought she was!

He brought her not only fruit and toast, but
bacon, eggs, mushrooms and waffles as well, and
stood over her while she ate them perched at the
counter in the dispensary.

She had just finished a delicious mangosteen when
Ben sauntered in, looking rumpled and as sexy as
sin.

She flushed, and Ah Seng smiled his secretive,
Oriental smile and removed her tray victoriously.

'Nice breakfast?' Ben asked.

She nodded 'Wonderful. I think Ah Seng's trying
to feed me up.'

'Too skinny,' Ah Seng commented.

'I think she's just right,' Ben corrected. 'Am I too
late?' he asked hopefully.

'You oversleep, Dr Ben? Your cabin very quiet
this morning.'

'Shut up, old man,' Ben told him fondly.

'How I supposed to wake you if not in your cabin?' Ah Seng asked him pointedly. 'What I supposed to do—bang on every cabin door?'

Maggie laughed softly. 'You knew where he was, you old fraud.'

'Not my job to go looking for him—if he want to behave like alley-cat, he miss breakfast,' Ah Seng said prudishly. 'However, under circumstances. . .'

He carried her tray out and left them alone.

'He's impossible,' Ben said with a chuckle.

'He reminds me of my grandmother,' Maggie told him drily.

'The one who's trying to marry you off?'

'The very same.'

'What a terrifying thought. I'm sorry I fell asleep on you, but it's probably just as well I did. How are our patients this morning?'

While they waited for Ben's breakfast Maggie gave him a quick report.

'Sounds good—just as long as they all remain stable until we get to Singapore. We should be there by lunchtime. I'll take you out for dinner tonight— local cuisine cooked by the roadside. If we can both stay awake, that is!'

They docked at one-thirty, and by three the paperwork had all been done and the patients were transferred to the Singapore General Hospital. The other members of the party went with them to undergo tests and for observation until the incubation period had elapsed, and Maggie stood at the quayside and watched them go.

Ben went with them to make sure that the doctor in charge had all the information he would need, and promised Maggie he would be back within an hour.

'Go and rest, you'll need lots of energy for what I've got in mind,' he warned with a laugh, and she watched him go with a feeling of trepidation. Had her reprieve come to an end? And did she care?

Frankly she was too tired to care. She made her way back down to her cabin and fell on to the bunk fully dressed.

Someone—probably Ah Seng—had tidied the bedclothes, but the pillow smelt faintly of Ben, and she snuggled her face into it and fell asleep in seconds.

'So, what would you like to do?'

Maggie shrugged her slim shoulders, totally bemused by all the sights and sounds that surrounded them.

'I have no idea—you tell me!'

'Do you want to shop? We could go to Orchard Road and buy all the duty-free goodies in the world, or we could go to the Botanic Gardens, or up Mount Faber and across to Sentosa Island on the cable car, then see the Butterfly Park and Undersea World and come back by ferry—that would take us up to this evening, then we could go and party—disco in a hotel, for instance—or somewhere quiet for dinner—it's up to you.'

Maggie was at a loss.

'The butterflies and the undersea place sound nice—and the cable car.'

'Fine—what about tonight?'

She looked up at him. 'Can we wait and see? We might be too tired to move by then.'

'No chance!' he said with a laugh. 'Are you ready?'

She nodded, her eyes bright despite her tiredness, and Ben laughed and hugged her to his side.

'Come on, then. Let's go.'

They travelled by air-conditioned taxi the half-mile or so from the World Trade Centre, where the *Island Pearl* was berthed, up to the cable car station at the top of Mount Faber, from where they had the most fabulous panoramic view of the harbour and city.

'There's the *Island Pearl* down there, and there's the hospital,' Ben told her, pointing to a building in the distance.

'I wondered where it was—are they all OK?'

'Should be—Mr Grey's a bit dodgy, but otherwise they're doing well. There's the harbour, and that's the Benjamin Sheares Bridge you crossed the Singapore River on.'

Maggie was amazed at the sheer size of the city.

'It's a real contrast of architectural styles, isn't it? Are all those tall buildings hotels?'

Ben smiled. 'Mostly. Odd, aren't they? Some round, some triangular, all trying to be more distinctive than the next. And yet it's the old architecture that really stands out. I'll take you up Emerald Hill later, if you want to see something really striking, after we have a Singapore Sling in Raffles, then we'll do Orchard Road and spend all that lovely money that's burning a hole in your pocket—OK?'

She laughed weakly. 'I just hope I've got the stamina for it!'

'We'll go everywhere by taxi—it'll be a breeze.'

And it was—starting with the cable car ride across

the water to the lovely little island of Sentosa, where
they visited the Butterfly Park and Undersea World,
then round to the ferry terminal on the monorail
high above the traffic.

It was sunset as they boarded the ferry for the
return trip, and the city was suddenly flooded with a
mass of twinkling lights. It was wonderfully romantic, and Maggie was headily conscious of Ben's
presence close by her side. As they arrived back in
the World Trade Centre, he suggested they should
go and shower and change for the evening.

'What should I wear?' she asked, unsure of how
formal an evening it would be.

'Something glamorous,' he said with a suggestive
twinkle, and Maggie's heart thudded against her
ribs.

Uncertain about the sense of doing what he suggested, she settled for the classic little black dress,
with the pearl stud earrings her grandmother had
given her and a pair of black strappy sandals. She
just hoped Ben meant what he said about taking
taxis everywhere, because as sure as eggs she
couldn't walk far in heels that high. She piled her
hair up on her head and tugged a few tendrils free,
then pouted at herself in the mirror.

'You'll do,' she advised herself with a last critical
glance at the dress.

Dead on time there was a knock on her cabin
door, and she opened it to admit Ben, formally
dressed in shirt and tie and dark trousers.

'All set?' he asked, and she nodded.

'Is this OK?'

He ran his eye over her simple dress. 'Very OK,
but you might be chilly later—have you got a wrap?'

'No, I. . .a cardigan?'

He shook his head. 'We'll find something in Orchard Road. Come on, time's a-wasting.'

With a touch of mock chivalry, he clicked his heels, bent forwards and extended his arm. 'Shall we?'

She laughed and scooped up her bag. 'Let's,' she said brightly, and took the proffered arm.

It was a hectic whirl, and the fabled Singapore Sling in the Long Bar at Raffles did nothing to steady her head.

'What's in this?' she asked, peering dubiously into the tall glass.

'Don't ask. It's a gin base.'

'And the rest,' she said drily, and drained the glass with a little giggle. 'Show me Singapore!' she said expansively.

So he took her up Emerald Hill, and showed her the old architecture, took her round Peranakan Place and pointed out the glorious plasterwork and ornate tiling, the soft greeny blues and yellows of the walls and shutters, the fabulously intricate screenwork above the windows, and then led her back down to Orchard Road.

'Oh, no, so much to buy!' she moaned, and Ben laughed.

'It's easy—and it doesn't hurt a bit!'

'I haven't got any money—can I change traveller's cheques? I should have thought of that.'

'No problem,' he said, and led her quickly through the seething throng to a money changer.

She found there was no language problem, and within minutes she had a handful of local currency and the world at her feet.

She bought a camera, after Ben had stopped her with a hand on her arm and haggled the price down to rock bottom in a strange tongue that seemed English and yet evidently wasn't always.

'What were you speaking?' she asked in amazement.

'Singlish—a sort of Singapore English. It's a funny old mixture of all sorts, but it's a very expressive way to communicate! Here,' he handed her the camera, 'let's look for a wrap, you'll be chilly later.'

They went up to Babazar Design Market on Cuppage Terrace, and she found an exquisitely carved Bali head that he insisted on buying for her as she'd had to forgo her visit to Bali because of the *legionella* outbreak.

Further on he found a shawl, an exquisite batik on silk in a vivid swirl of jewel colours, and draped it gently round her shoulders.

'It suits you—do you like it?'

She nodded speechlessly. His hands were warm and firm against her arms, and he was looking into her eyes with a mixture of tenderness and desire that made her knees go weak.

His fingers traced the hollow of her throat. 'You could do with something round your neck—come on, I know just the place.'

He led her through the crowd to a side street, and into a little shop where the Chinese proprietor was perched on a stool at the back, hunched over a watch that he was repairing.

'Lee Chung—how goes, old man?'

'Ben! Can do, *la*—what today?'

Once again Ben broke into rapid Singlish, and

Maggie stood bemused as the man produced a tray of pearl necklaces.

'Ben, you can't——'

'Hush. Lee Chung, this rubbish, *la*.'

'Now-then you say!'

The man disappeared grumbling into the back of the shop, and appeared again a moment later with a small, flat box.

He opened it with a flourish, and Ben nodded.

'Better. *Berapa harga, la*?'

Once again the incomprehensible wrangling commenced, and moments later he handed over a credit card and picked up the string of pearls.

They were smaller than the others, but simpler, and Maggie was delighted. She imagined Ben had persuaded the man to produce the less expensive pearls that he didn't usually display in the shop, and was relieved at his common sense, because the price tickets on the displayed necklaces made her blood curdle.

The pearls felt cool against her skin, and the brush of Ben's fingers against the nape of her neck was intoxicating.

He fastened the clip and turned her back to face him.

'Lovely. Thank you, Lee Chung. Goodnight.'

The old man replied in Singlish with a wicked wheezy chuckle, and then Ben was taking her back to the hustle and bustle of Orchard Road.

'What did he say?' Maggie asked, eyeing Ben's slightly reddened neck with interest.

Ben laughed.

'Nothing for your ears, my love. Come on—time to feed you up.'

'Tell me!' she insisted.

'No. Suffice it to say it was a compliment.'

'Then you could tell me——'

'I could, but I wouldn't dream of it. You'd be mortally embarrassed, and so would I.'

'Good grief, it must have been quite something!'

He smiled wryly. 'It was. Now give me all those things to carry and let's go and eat. I'm ravenous.'

'Where are we going?'

'Depends. Do you want a sophisticated meal in elegant surroundings, or local colour and something more basic?'

'Local colour,' she replied promptly. 'I've had *haute cuisine* up to here on the ship—I could do with something a little different!'

Ben chuckled. 'I shall pass on your views to the management. In the meantime, we'll go to a food centre and buy hawker food and eat it on the pavement—OK?'

Two hours later Maggie was groaning.

'I thought it was going to be something simple!' she wailed.

'You didn't have to eat everything,' he teased gently.

'Look,' she told him, pointing a slim forefinger at his chest, 'I won't be doing this again. I didn't want to miss out on anything!'

He laughed. 'I lived in Singapore for fifteen years, and I still haven't tried everything. Only you would try and cram it all into one night!'

'Not quite all,' she replied, pretending to be insulted.

'Almost. Come on, we ought to be getting back to the ship. She sails in an hour.'

In the confines of the air-conditioned taxi, wined, dined and with her mind whirling with gaily coloured images, Maggie snuggled up to Ben and sighed.

What was it Jo Carter had said to her? Something about the last time she had spent the evening with someone she had really liked, and Maggie had wondered if she ever had. All that was changed now, thanks to Ben.

'Thank you for a wonderful evening,' she mumbled.

'You're welcome,' he replied, his lips brushing her forehead as his arm came round her to hug her to his side.

'You shouldn't have bought me those pearls— you're very naughty,' she said sleepily.

'Rubbish. Think of them as a thank-you for all the help you've given me. They'll help to remind you of the ship.'

'I'll have to pay you back.'

His lips nuzzled her hair. 'I'll only take payment in kind.'

She giggled. 'That'll take a lifetime, and we've only got a few more nights.'

'We'll have to make the best of them, won't we?' he murmured, and then the taxi drew up at the quayside and Ben was helping her up the gangway to the *Island Pearl*.

Minutes later he opened her cabin door and followed her in, taking her gently into his arms.

She yawned and snuggled into his chest, her eyes drooping.

Beneath her ear she heard a chuckle in his chest.

'I think you'd better get to bed, my little mermaid. I've kept you up long enough.'

She lifted her head sleepily and frowned slightly at him.

'You can't go.'

'But I can—I am.'

'But—I thought. . .'

Ben gave a rueful grin. 'When I make love to you, I shall expect you to be alert and paying attention, and at the moment I don't think you'd stay awake if I put on the most startling performance of my career!'

'You do yourself a disservice,' she mumbled, and yawned again.

He laughed softly. 'I think not. Goodnight, my darling. Sleep well. I'll see you tomorrow.'

He dropped a chaste kiss on her lips and left her wondering how she was going to stay awake long enough to undress.

If he'd stayed, of course, he would have done it for her and saved her the trouble.

She giggled tiredly. Oh, well. One night in her clothes wouldn't hurt.

She toppled on to her bunk, her fingers curled round her pearls, and fell instantly asleep.

CHAPTER FIVE

'HELLO, darling! Long time no see—I thought he must have chucked you overboard!'

Maggie laughed. 'Hello, Rhoda. Sorry to abandon you, I've been rather busy helping Ben with his patients.'

Rhoda patted the chair beside her. 'Come and join me for breakfast and tell me all about it. I think you've been simply wonderful helping out like that, you know. He was very lucky to have you on board—but how about your holiday? You haven't had any rest at all!'

'Oh, I had a lovely day yesterday—he took me all round Singapore and we had a wonderful time.'

Rhoda sipped her coffee and eyed Maggie over the top. 'Fallen in a big way, haven't you, sweetheart?'

Maggie stared thoughtfully at her hand for a moment, then she looked up and smiled at Rhoda.

'Yes, I suppose I have,' she said gently. 'I thought he was a playboy, but I'm not sure any more. I think there's a lot more to him than meets the eye, but he doesn't talk much about himself so it's difficult to find out what!'

Rhoda gave a tinkling laugh. 'Don't knock it, dearie. The last thing you want is a man who talks about himself all the time—take my word for it! My last lover was *awful*—nearly drove me insane with

84

his self-centred conversation. And God knows there
was precious little to talk about!'

Maggie chuckled. 'Anyway, the patients are all
safely delivered to the hospital in Singapore now, so
we can relax for the remainder of the cruise.'

'Good. Now, how about some breakfast?'

'No! Oh, no—I ate so much last night I don't
think I'm ever going to want food again. Coffee at
the outside.'

When they had finished, they made their way out
on deck to the sunbeds and found a shady spot in
the lee of the wind. They were steaming up the west
coast of Malaysia, and Maggie lay back and watched,
fascinated, as the scenery fluctuated from bustling
port to waving palms and back again.

Rhoda disappeared mid-morning for a swim, and
a few moments later Maggie's view was interrupted
by a pair of tanned hairy knees.

She glanced up, a smile ready on her face, and it
faltered at the intensity of Ben's gaze.

'Dear God, you are so beautiful,' he murmured,
and, perching on Rhoda's sunbed, he reached out
for Maggie's hand. 'How are you today?'

She smiled. 'Fantastic. I slept like a log—I'm
sorry about last night, but you were absolutely right.
I couldn't even be bothered to undress!'

His thumb made lazy circles on the soft skin on
the underside of her wrist as his eyes tracked slowly
over her near-nakedness. She was suddenly pulsat-
ingly aware of the brevity of her bikini and the
almost overwhelming urge to remove it and any
other barriers between them.

'You be sure to get plenty of rest today,' he said

huskily, and with a slow, sexy wink he straightened up and left her, almost moaning with frustration.

He appeared again at lunchtime, and joined her for a buffet at the poolside before going back down to the medical centre for a routine surgery at two.

She joined Rhoda and a middle-aged couple from Surrey for a game of deck quoits, and then she had a quick dip before heading back to her cabin.

Ben caught her on the way in and followed her through the door, pushing it shut behind him.

'Alone at last!' he said theatrically, and she giggled somewhat nervously.

'Are you busy?' he asked her.

'No, I was just going to have a shower and lie down for a while in the cool.'

'I've got a better idea. I can scrape an hour off— how about relaxing in the sauna and jacuzzi for a while?'

'Where is it?'

'Next deck down—there's a swimming-pool and fitness-room and all sorts of things. You'd better wear a bikini; it's open to anyone. Fancy it?'

She nodded. 'Great—sounds really relaxing. Do they have a cold plunge?'

He chuckled. 'Oh, yes. Definitely! Have a quick shower, and I'll see you outside my cabin in a minute.'

He left her while she showered and twisted her hair up into a bun, then, taking her towel and wearing her bikini and a wrap, she made her way to his cabin.

He was ready for her, sitting on the bed in a towelling robe that stopped halfway down his thighs. She felt a shiver run through her as he stood up and reached out to take her hand. 'Are you ready?' he murmured, and she could only nod, bereft of her powers of speech.

The fitness centre was extremely well equipped, and they hung up their things and went first into the steam-room, where the atmosphere was suffocatingly hot and the steam scented with aromatic oils. It was impossible to see across the room, and Maggie had to feel her way to the bench round the side wall, but nevertheless she was supremely conscious of his superb physique and near-nakedness. The brief glimpse of him in slim black trunks before they had entered the steam-room had been more than enough.

'Are you OK?' he asked. 'It can be a bit much until you're used to it.'

She sat beside him on the bench and sighed. 'Wonderful. There's a place near where I work that I go to sometimes with a friend. It's so relaxing.'

'Mmm.' His hand slid along the bench and his fingers intertwined with hers in silent companionship.

How wonderful, she thought, and had a momentary pang that it was all destined to be so brief. Only two more whole days—and three nights—and she would be flying home, leaving him forever. She wondered if she would ever see him again, and stifled the pang of misery that wrenched through her.

She would take what she was given, and be thankful for it.

Ben nudged her. 'I've had enough.'

'Me, too.' She stood up carefully, and groped her way to the door. It was blissfully cool outside, and they sank gratefully into the icy water of the cold plunge.

Then they lay for several minutes being pummelled by the warm jets of the jacuzzi, and then went into the sauna, enduring the dry heat until they felt dizzy and headed back out into the cool.

After a couple of circuits they finished up with the jacuzzi, and Maggie felt so relaxed that she wasn't sure she could drag herself out of the water.

They had the place to themselves, and Ben lay across the whirlpool from her, his feet rubbing lazily up and down her calves.

'Better?' he asked sensuously.

'Oh, much. I feel like a boneless cat—actually, I don't think I can stand,' she confessed with a laugh.

Ben rose to his feet and plucked her effortlessly from the water, cradling her against his chest as he stepped out of the tub.

The warm water streaming from their bodies pooled, trapped between them where her side met the hard, taut muscles of his abdomen. The light scatter of hair on his chest curled damply on the skin, and she traced the path of a trickle with her fingertip, drawing a groan from him.

'I hope you're going to be wide awake later,' he murmured threateningly, and she giggled and tweaked one of the curls.

'Ow! Little wretch. I'll get you back for that after dinner,' he promised.

'You and whose army?' she asked cheekily, and he quirked a brow.

'Fighting talk, eh? We'll see.'

He set her down on her feet, handed her her towel and pulled on his robe.

They walked back to Java Deck and he left her at her cabin door with the brush of his lips on her brow.

'I'll deal with you later,' he said softly.

'Oh, promises, promises!' she teased.

'You'd better believe it!' he laughed, and walked away, his stride confident.

Maggie watched him till he reached his cabin door, and then waved before going into her cabin.

Her reprieve was definitely over, and not a moment too soon.

She dressed carefully for dinner, and was gratified to see his carefully controlled reaction when he entered the Frangipani Room a few moments after her.

'You,' he murmured for her ears only, 'are asking for trouble, and you're going to damn well get it!'

She smiled mischievously. 'Thank you. I think you look pretty special too.'

He chuckled. 'Allow me to escort you to your place, Dr Wells.'

He seated her courteously, and throughout the meal he behaved with the utmost propriety.

Only Maggie was aware of their feet intertwined, and the subtle pressure of his thigh against hers.

'Don't overeat,' he warned wickedly in an undertone.

His advice was unnecessary. Her appetite had deserted her, and it seemed to take the greatest effort to swallow past the pounding of her heart.

When the meal was finally over, he led her through the Penang Lounge and out on deck, there taking her in his arms to the soft strains of the palm court band.

They moved only slightly, their bodies close, their hearts beating in unison, and when Ben lifted his head and whispered her name she could only nod in response.

He hugged her briefly, then slipped his arm around her shoulders and led her back to the lift.

It was crowded, as before, and he smiled and chatted with the passengers as befitted his position as an officer of the ship's company.

As he followed her through her cabin door, however, his smile slipped and he became just a man, haunted by a passion that turned his eyes to flame.

Maggie watched, spellbound, as he turned the lock. The click was deafening in the quiet room, and as they stood facing each other she was conscious of everything about him—the breadth of his shoulders, his height, the way his hair fell forward on to his brow. The subtle scent of his cologne, mixed with something that was distinctly Ben, drifted in the still air and taunted her senses.

He was waiting, she realised finally, for her to make the first move, but her body seemed frozen and beyond her control.

As the seconds dragged out into minutes, she began to shake, her whole body trembling with the force of need that suddenly engulfed her.

'Hold me,' she whispered, and then she was in his arms and he was rocking her, his voice soft, his arms firm about her, his body trembling against her.

'It's OK,' he told her gently. 'We don't have to do anything you don't want.'

'But I want it all,' she said raggedly, and then he was kissing her wildly, passionately, and his body shuddered as he fought to contain his need.

Whimpering, she tugged at his clothes, and he shed his jacket and shirt and her hands were skittering over his skin, desperate to touch him.

He eased away from her and stripped to his briefs, then turned her round so that he could unfasten the back of her dress. Turning her back, he eased it down over her shoulders and let it fall to the floor, leaving her in nothing but a scrap of silk. As Maggie watched, his eyes closed and he sucked in his breath sharply. Then his eyes opened again, and he reached out a hand as if to touch her.

'You're so beautiful,' he breathed, and let his eyes feast slowly on her body.

She closed her eyes, unable to bear his scrutiny, and then she felt the gentle brush of his knuckles against her cheek.

'Don't be embarrassed,' he murmured. 'This is me, Maggie. Let me see you.'

Her eyes flickered open and met his, and the look in them nearly took her breath away.

Opening her arms, she reached out and clung to him, unable to bear the space between them any more.

'Make love to me, Ben,' she pleaded, and then he lifted her and laid her gently on her bunk, coming down beside her so that his body lay hard against her side, the rough texture of his chest and thighs in delicious contrast to the smooth firmness of her ripe young body.

The last scraps of clothing dispensed with, he bent his head to kiss her, and her hand strayed to his hip, revelling in the sharp angles and smooth curves of his masculine frame.

His hand cupped her breast, teasing the nipple to

vibrant life, then wandered slowly down her flank, over the curve of her hip, to caress the soft skin of her inner thigh.

She moaned against his mouth, and his hand moved up to touch her with even greater intimacy as his lips trailed over her jaw, down past the hollow of her throat to her breast. As his mouth closed hotly over the aching peak, she let out a tiny cry of ecstasy and writhed against him, desperate to obliterate the last infinitesimal distance between them.

He turned away from her, fumbling with something in his jacket, and it was several seconds before she realised what he was doing. No doubt later she would be glad that one of them had had some wits about them, but just then she was shaken with a need so great that her thoughts were almost incoherent.

'Please, Ben,' she moaned, and then he was moving over her, lowering himself down gently on to her to accustom her to his weight, and then with one long, slow thrust he entered her.

The pain of his possession was nothing compared to the joy of this exquisite union, and with a glad cry she wound herself around him and clung to him.

Her body, as if by instinct, followed his lead and joined the age-old ritual, and as she reached the peak and tumbled headlong his arms were there to catch her as he shuddered against her, her name a hoarse cry on his lips.

'Hi.'

Maggie blinked sleepily and then blushed. 'Hi yourself. Is it morning?'

'Nearly. We've just docked at Penang.'

'Oh.' She dropped her eyes, unable to deal with the tumble of emotions racing through her. Was he going to ignore the stupendous events of the night before? It seemed impossible, pressed together as they were from shoulder to ankle by the narrow confines of her bunk, and yet——

'About last night. . .'

Oh, no, she thought, he's going to say it was a mistake and let's be friends or something awful and I'm going to cry and make a fool of myself.

'What about it?'

'Why me?'

'What?'

'I said, why me? Or did I dream it? I just got the distinct impression it was your first time, and I wondered why you chose me.'

Because I love you, she wanted to say, but thought better of it.

'It just seemed the natural thing to do—anyway, after twenty-eight years virginity is a bit of a burden. I'm sorry—was it very boring for you? You'll have to tell me what to do——'

'Idiot.' He hugged her tight, wrapping her in his arms and holding her firmly against his broad, solid chest. 'It was far from boring—in fact, I find I can't wait to repeat the experience.'

He lifted her chin and kissed her tenderly. 'Are you sore?'

She blushed again. 'I don't think so.'

'I'll be gentle—stop me if I hurt you.'

But he didn't, and his patience and tenderness, coupled with fiercely controlled passion, reduced her to tears of joy in his arms.

He kissed the tears away and curled her into his arms, sighing with contentment.

'Oh, Maggie, that was so special,' he murmured, and she fell asleep with the sound of his heart a reassuring beat against her ear.

When they woke again it was daylight, and they showered and dressed—Maggie in a calf-length cotton skirt and T-shirt, Ben in his dress shirt and trousers—and she checked that it was clear before he slipped out and went along to his cabin to change.

He appeared at her cabin door a few minutes later in casual cotton trousers and a polo shirt, and winked at her. 'Got away with that, thank God. I must just pop into the medical centre and make sure that Ah Seng knows I'm going ashore—if anyone needs a doctor they can call one from the island.'

Maggie was a little surprised. 'Can you do that?'

He grinned wickedly. 'I'm doing it! Come on, the day'll be gone. We'll have breakast in Georgetown.'

They took a trishaw, a sort of tricycle with a buggy attached, pedalled by a hunched little man in a coolie hat, and wove through the streets of Chinatown. Ben pointed out the sights as they went, and then they arrived at the Eastern and Oriental Hotel, one of the oldest hotels on the island.

There they took breakfast on the terrace overlooking the sea, and then visited the Botanical Gardens. The colourful profusion of foliage and flowers was set in an enchanted valley, and Maggie was delighted by the antics of the cheeky little rhesus monkeys.

'I wonder what they would think if they knew of their contribution to haematology?' Maggie mused, and Ben laughed wryly.

'Probably not much. You can't eat it or swing from it!'

Laughing, they strolled together hand in hand back to the gate.

'Where now?' she asked her knowledgeable guide, and he shrugged.

'Temple?'

'Why not?'

After they had seen the awe-inspiring Temple of the Reclining Buddha, the midday sun was beginning to overwhelm Maggie, so they took the funicular railway to the cool heights of Penang Hill.

They saw pitcher plants hanging, their pendulous traps agape, and orchids and ferns growing out of the walls of the cutting as the car ground its way slowly to the top. Once there they wandered slowly past the old colonial bungalows, and marvelled at the superb views of the mainland in the distance. The Penang Bridge, the longest in South-East Asia, arched across to Butterworth, and beneath them they could see the colourful spread of Georgetown with the harbour beyond.

It was wonderfully cool, and they were surrounded by lush vegitation thriving in the cooler atmosphere.

They lunched on fruit which they purchased by the roadside, and then made their way back down on the funicular railway to the hot, intense hubbub of Georgetown. They shopped in the old town, walking side by side on the covered walkways protected from the worst of the sun, and then returned to the E and O for afternoon tea.

'We'll have dinner in Gurney Drive—native fare cooked by the road,' Ben told her. 'They aren't as commercial as Singapore, but the food's just as delicious.'

Maggie sighed with contentment. 'Sounds marvellous, but I'll need to freshen up a bit—it's awfully hot.'

'Come on, then.' Ben rose to his feet, held her chair and led her out, hailing a taxi from outside the hotel.

Once back at the ship they made their way down to Java Deck, and went straight to Maggie's cabin.

'Who's going to shower first, you or me?' she asked Ben.

His mouth curled into a wicked smile. 'I have a better idea.' He shrugged off his shirt, kicked off his shoes, and peeled off Maggie's clothes, ignoring her laughing protest.

'We'll save water,' he explained. 'The desalination plant doesn't work in dock.'

'Is that right?'

'I have no idea, but it seems reasonable,' he said, and she chuckled and went into his arms.

Much later they dressed and headed up in the lift to the main deck.

'I'm starving!' she confessed.

'Remember Singapore,' he teased, 'although I could imagine you would be hungry—you've just used up a colossal amount of energy!'

She blushed, and he hugged her to his side with a chuckle. 'Don't be shy, you were wonderful,' he murmured, and the lift doors opened and they were making their way out into the colourful night.

Forewarned by her experience in Singapore,

Free Books and Gifts claim

Yes Please send me my 4 FREE Temptation romances together with my FREE gifts. Please also reserve a special Reader Service subscription for me. If I decide to subscribe, I will receive 4 superb new Temptations for just £7.00 every month, post and packing FREE. If I decide not to subscribe I shall write to you within 10 days. The FREE books and gifts will be mine to keep. I understand that I am under no obligation whatsoever. I may cancel or suspend my subscription at any time simply by writing to you. I am over 18 years of age.

1A3T

Name _____

Address _____

_____

_____ Postcode _____

Signature _____

Mills & Boon Reader Service
FREEPOST
P.O. Box 236
Croydon
CR9 9EL

Send NO money now

NO STAMP NEEDED

Maggie ate with restraint and tried just a few dishes, sharing them with Ben.

They fed each other tasty morsels, and as the tension built between them they took a trishaw back to the ship and made love again far into the night, while the ship left the harbour and started the return trip to Singapore

The next day Ben was run off his feet, dealing with tummy upsets from injudicious culinary experiments, insect bites and sunstroke, so Maggie spent the day on deck with Rhoda, dozing fitfully and trying to forget that this time tomorrow it would all be over and she would be on her way home, her love-affair with Ben a thing of the past.

He joined her for lunch, chatting easily with the passengers and laughing at their dreadful jokes, and every now and then he would wink at Maggie or brush his hand accidentally against her thigh, and she would fight the urge to blush at the direction of her thoughts.

Dinner was spectacular, but all she could think of was that it was their last dinner together, and she would never see him again.

That night their lovemaking held a kind of gentle desperation, a yearning tenderness born of parting, and they slept locked in each other's arms, to wake again and again, driven by the inexorable passage of time to taste the sweet wine of passion.

Then it was dawn, and the engines fell silent for the last time. Maggie turned her head into Ben's shoulder and wept.

'Don't cry,' he murmured, 'this isn't goodbye, Maggie. It's my last tour—I'll be back in England in a week and I'll get in touch, I promise.'

'It won't be the same,' she whispered brokenly, and he laughed, a little unsteadily.

'No, hopefully we'll have a bigger bed. I mean it, darling—this isn't finished, not by a long way.'

'We'll be miles apart,' she said miserably.

'Wait and see. We'll work something out.'

He lowered his head and kissed her tenderly, and she wrapped her arms around him and hugged him as if she would never let him go. Then a tap came on the cabin door.

'Dr Ben—patient for you,' Ah Seng said quietly, and Ben groaned.

'Bloody awful timing that man has!'

Maggie released him reluctantly. 'You have to go.'

'Mmm. I'll see you in the medical centre in a few minutes.'

He dressed quickly, and when he had gone Maggie showered and dressed in her travelling clothes, packing a change of warm clothing in a carry-on bag for her arrival in England. Then when everything was ready she let herself out of her cabin.

As she did so she caught a fleeting glimpse of a tall, willowy blonde with stunning legs and an enviably lush figure, entering the medical centre, and as she approached she could hear Ben's startled exclamation and the laughter of the woman. As she stepped into the doorway she saw him throw his arms round her and hug her.

'Jan, what on earth are you doing here?' he asked, his voice a mixture of delight and confusion.

He held her at arm's length and studied her face intently. 'There's nothing wrong, is there?'

'Good lord, no, just checking up on you, you old rogue. Got any objections?'

'Of course not—it's wonderful to see you.'

She stroked his cheek with the familiarity of possession, and Maggie pressed her fingers to her lips.

'You look tired—I heard about the problems.'

'Oh, Jan, it was—God, I could have done with you here.' He pulled her into a hug, and Maggie pressed her hand harder over her mouth to stop herself from crying out. So all the time she had been a substitute. . .

The woman laughed and hugged him back. 'Sorry I was busy. I've decided we're getting married on the day before Valentine's Day—I take it you're free?'

'Free?' He laughed in delight. 'How could I not be free? Oh, Jan, that's fantastic—at last! How long have I been trying to talk you into doing this?'

'Years, I think! Oh, Ben, I'm so happy!'

'Me, too. I can't think why it took you so long—I knew straight away! Oh, Jan, I'm so pleased——'

Maggie didn't stop to listen to any more. Her heart in tatters, she fled back to her cabin, picked up her luggage and made her way to the lift.

Ah Seng stepped out as the doors opened, and frowned at her. 'Dr Maggie going?'

She conjured a weak smile. 'I think so. Dr Ben's busy—say goodbye to him for me, would you, and tell him—tell him I hope he'll be very happy?'

She left the startled steward standing open-mouthed and pressed the button for the main deck. There she found the purser and told him she would be making her own arrangements to get to Changi airport, if he could transport her luggage for her, and then she left the ship that had been her home for the past week and a half and stepped on to the quayside, hailing a taxi to take her almost anywhere but here, the scene of her betrayal.

As they pulled away she glanced up and saw the brightly coloured cable cars swinging their way across from Mount Faber to Sentosa Island, and she was flooded with memories of Ben—Ben laughing, Ben teasing her, Ben holding her in his arms and making tender, passionate love to her. . .and then Ben, his arms around a beautiful, elegant woman who in five weeks' time would apparently become his bride.

CHAPTER SIX

MAGGIE gave herself precisely twenty-four hours to get over the flight and her reaction to Ben's infidelity, then she donned her stethoscope and white coat and threw herself back into the fray.

Not, however, before she had found a photo shop and had all the photos of Ben developed that she had taken with her new camera, and wept buckets over each one in turn, and not before she had had a bitter argument with Lucinda, who turned up, ears positively flapping, a few hours after Maggie arrived back on the Friday morning.

'Was it wonderful?' she asked hopefully.

Maggie couldn't be bothered with tact.

'No,' she replied. 'It was bloody awful.'

'Oh, darling! I had so hoped you'd get on with him. I had such visions of you falling for him. . .'

Maggie snorted. 'Well, let me tell you, Grannie, darling, you succeeded beyond your wildest imaginings. Unfortunately the faithless rat is nothing more than a promiscuous playboy, and I hope I never see him again in my life!'

At which point she burst into tears and made an undignified exit.

Sunday morning at eight o'clock saw her in the thick of things in SCBU. It was the tenth of January, less than two weeks since her departure, and she marvelled at how the stable, even course of her life could have been so derailed in so short a time.

Peter Travers smiled absently at her as she walked on to the ward, muttered something about 'Nice holiday?' and floated off, his nose in a set of notes.

'No,' she muttered crossly, 'I didn't have a nice holiday.'

Coupled with her misery, the weather was appalling, cold, sleeting constantly, with the result that her flat was freezing and it was impossible to sleep— not that the cold made much difference, because she was fairly sure she wouldn't sleep anyway.

Every time she lay down and closed her eyes, she saw Ben, and her arms ached to hold him. When she opened her eyes the images were gone, replaced with cold, lonely reality. Frankly she wasn't sure which was worse, and positively longed for the nights on duty when she could stay at the hospital and work herself into the ground.

Amy had been discharged into the care of foster parents, and so Maggie was able to avoid Jo in SCBU for the first day, but then she bumped into Jo and Anne in the canteen on Monday and could no longer avoid their penetrating questions.

'Well?' Jo asked immediately. 'Was it the captain?'

Maggie smiled brightly. 'No, it wasn't the captain, it was the ship's doctor.'

'And?' Annie prompted.

'And nothing,' Maggie said breezily. 'He was fun, we danced, and mostly we nursed passengers with legionnaires' disease——'

'What?' they chorused, and so Maggie was able to get off the subject of Ben and on to the subject of their patients—for a while.

'So what happened after you got rid of them at

Singapore?' Jo persisted. 'Did he wine and dine you and—so on?'

They all laughed—all except Maggie.

Then Jo caught Annie's eye and shrugged.

'I think,' she said, patting Maggie's hand, 'we ought to get together for a long chat.'

'I don't want to talk about it,' Maggie mumbled.

'A problem shared, and all that—how about this evening at my place?' Anne suggested. 'Beth goes to bed at seven-thirty, so we'd be on our own. We could have a Chinese take-away——'

'No!' Maggie begged, suddenly flooded with memories of eating Chinese food with Ben in Singapore at a roadside stall in Newton. 'Fish and chips, Indian, anything but Chinese—please?'

'OK, Indian,' they agreed, and she sighed with relief.

'Got any photos?' Jo asked, and so she took her photos of Singapore—Ben eating with chopsticks, Ben laughing in the trishaw, Ben standing on the deck of the *Island Pearl*—and Penang—Ben on the terrace at the E and O, Ben and the rhesus monkeys, Ben on the top of Penang Hill with the view of the mainland in the distance, Ben holding a colourful length of batik cloth, Ben, Ben, Ben—always Ben.

'He is rather beautiful,' Jo said quietly. 'So what happened?'

'He's apparently already involved with someone else, and now he's getting married on the thirteenth of February—the day before Valentine's Day. Isn't that romantic?'

'Unlucky for some,' Annie murmured sympathetically.

Jo was appalled. 'What did he say about it? God, the rat!'

'He didn't say anything. I overheard him talking to her.'

'And you didn't confront him?'

Maggie laughed without humour. 'Hardly. They were wrapped in a clinch at the time—it wouldn't have been very pleasant for any of us if I'd gone up to him and said, "Congratulations—aren't you going to introduce me to your fiancée?"'

Her voice cracked on the last word and she crammed the photos back into the envelope and shoved them into her bag.

'Oh, dear,' Jo commiserated. 'Between the legionnaires' and the ship's rat, you had rather a raw deal really, didn't you?'

Maggie snorted. 'Enough about me. How about you?'

Jo shrugged. 'Oh, Amy's gone to a foster mother.'

'When did she go?'

'Last Monday—a week ago. I've seen her twice— Barbara's been very good, but I can't keep going round there all the time, and anyway we've been very busy at work. One of the other obs and gynae consultants has been off with flu and so Alex's workload has increased hugely, and, to be honest, we really need the time together. I wish we'd had time for a honeymoon. Sometimes I feel I hardly know him, and I see so little of him I wonder if I ever will.'

'You ought to get away together—isn't there any way you can manage it?' Anne asked.

Jo smiled bleakly. 'That would leave you awfully short-handed in the department, old love.'

Anne laughed. 'I'm sure you could find a locum to cover just for a couple of weeks. And anyway, what will happen when they say you can have Amy?'

'If,' Jo corrected her. 'Let's not jump the gun, we still don't know for sure.'

'If, then—what will happen? You'll have to get someone. And you ought to have time to keep in touch with Amy, because when—sorry, if—they give you the green light, she'll need to be used to you before you take her away from Barbara and bring her home.'

'Will you give up work when—if—you adopt her?' Maggie asked quietly.

'Oh, yes—she'll need all my love and attention if she's to thrive. She's still not a well baby, Maggie. Sometimes I'm so worried for her.'

Maggie squeezed Jo's hand. 'She'll be fine. Don't fret, Jo. She's a gutsy little thing.'

'But she's so small!'

'Rubbish! She's huge compared to some of the very low birthweight babies we treat successfully in that unit. All she needs is loads of TLC, and I'm sure she's getting it with Barbara. She's very experienced with special care babies.'

'I know,' Jo agreed wearily, 'but I wish she was with me. I love her so much, and I'm sure she knows it. . .'

They sat in silence for a moment, all busy with their thoughts, and then Anne pushed back her chair and switched on the kettle.

'Who's for a game of cards?'

'How about Cheat?' Maggie suggested wryly.

* * *

The week passed, slowly but surely. Maggie thought that as the days went it would get easier, but in the end she decided she just got used to the pain.

Work was busy, and because of the cold there were lots of chest infections and sickly, ailing children.

She was on call all weekend, and by Monday she was run ragged.

Then during the course of the morning she was called to A and E to look at a young girl with a broken arm.

As she walked into the unit, she could hear a woman crying, 'But I didn't hit her hard, I know I didn't!'

Maggie popped her head round Sister's office door. 'Hi, Kathleen. You wanted me?'

'Oh, yes, hi, Maggie. Shut the door.'

Maggie complied, and the little Irish sister handed her some X-rays. 'The new SR picked this up—four-year-old girl, not terribly bright by all accounts, mother thumped her this morning. She's on the non-accidental injury register, and the at-risk register, and Social Services have been keeping an eye for a time, but the mother seems very loving. Funny, isn't it, how they can be all over them one minute and beating hell out of them the next?'

Maggie shoved the X-ray up into the light box and squinted at it.

'It's not her first fracture, is it?'

'No—she's had one other on that arm, and an arm and leg when she was eighteen months—fell off the bed, apparently.' Kathleen's tone was sceptical.

Maggie tugged off the X-ray and opened the door. 'Let's have a look at her—where is she?'

'Cubicle three—the new SR's in there. I'll come—damn.' She reached for the ringing phone. 'Go and introduce yourself. I'll be with you in a minute. A and E, Sister speaking.'

Maggie left her dealing with the caller and walked briskly down to cubicle three.

She twitched open the curtain, and then froze in her tracks.

The little girl was sitting up on the examination couch in her vest and pants, her eyes like saucers, while a tall, fair man ran his hands gently over her legs.

He glanced under his arm, saw a white coat and straightened, turning as he did so.

'Ah, you must be—— Maggie!'

She felt the blood drain from her head, and steadied herself against the partition. Of all the conniving, devious women——

'Hello, Ben. You must be Bron's replacement.'

'That's right.' His eyes, those lovely, searching grey-blue eyes, scanned her pale face, and then he smiled with all the remembered warmth. 'Fancy seeing you here, of all places.'

She shrugged herself away from the wall, and mentally cursed her grandmother all the way to hell and back. 'Fancy,' she said drily. 'And of course you had no idea I would be here.'

'Of course not—we never got as far as discussing where you worked—as I recall, we always got distracted before we reached that point.' His laughing eyes tracked slowly over her face. 'It's good to see you again,' he said quietly.

'You said you'd be in touch—you must have known where to find me somehow.'

He sighed and ran his hand through his hair. 'I was going to get your address from the shipping line head office.'

'Hmph.' She turned away from him towards the child on the examination couch. 'So this is Petra, right? Hello, Petra. I'm Maggie. What happened, sweetheart?'

She perched on a chair that brought her face to the same level as the child's, and smiled encouragingly. Not for a moment could she allow the child to see the turmoil that raged inside her.

'Mummy smacked me,' she said slowly and not very distinctly.

'Were you naughty? I used to be naughty.'

'Not naughty,' Petra denied, and slow, heavy tears started down her cheeks.

Maggie brushed them gently away, then clicked her fingers near Petra's left ear. She didn't respond.

'She's got a history,' Ben murmured.

'I know that,' Maggie all but snapped, and then closed her eyes while she got control of herself again. 'Sorry. It's just. . .'

'I know. About Petra. . .'

Maggie nodded. 'She's had three previous fractures that we know of, and lots of welfare supervision, but I can't help feeling—has she had a hearing test?'

'A hearing test?'

'Yes, you know, when they test for hearing loss.'

'I know what a hearing test is,' Ben replied shortly. 'I just wondered why?'

'Deafness is often a symptom of osteogenesis imperfecta—brittle bone disease. It's often undetected in mild cases, and where there's an apparent

pattern of abuse the parents can get blamed for quite
honest accidents. In this case the mother obviously
hit Petra, but quite possibly not very hard. We'll
need her in for a day or two to investigate, and I
suppose the Social Services ought to be informed,
but look—can you see the whites of her eyes? The
sclera are so thin they appear almost blue. That's
another sign.'

Ben nodded slowly. 'Do you want to talk to the
mother? She's pretty distracted.'

'I'd better. We'll arrange to admit Petra and then
go from there.' Maggie turned back to the little girl
with a smile. 'Right, darling, we're going to arrange
for someone to put a plaster on your arm to stop it
hurting, and then we're going to let you stay here in
hospital for a few days while we try and find out
what's the matter—OK?'

Petra nodded, her eyes huge.

'Right, I'll get a nurse to stay with her and then
we'll talk to Mum. Is she in the interview-room?'

She called a junior nurse, and then headed off
towards the offices. Ben stopped her progress down
the corridor with a gentle but firm hand on her arm.

'Why did you run away?'

She studied his face for a moment, and then shook
her head on a slight laugh.

'Let's just say it was time to go.'

'You didn't say goodbye.'

She looked away. 'I hate goodbyes. Ben, we must
sort out that child.'

'Later, then—can I take you out for dinner
tonight?'

She almost laughed. 'Ben, I hardly think that
would be appropriate in the circumstances.'

He looked bewildered. It was almost convincing. 'What circumstances?'

'Oh, come on——! Look, Ben, it was nice while it lasted, but it's over, OK? Finished.'

'That's not what you said.'

'No—that's not what *you* said.'

'Don't split hairs, Maggie. What changed your mind?'

She closed her eyes, and saw again the tall, willowy blonde in his arms. 'Let's just say I discovered you're not my type after all.'

'That's rubbish, and you know it.'

She glared at him, her sense of justice well and truly riled. 'No, it isn't rubbish. It's the truth, and if your ego can't take it, well, I'm sorry, but there's nothing I either can or will do about it. It was a holiday romance, and it's over.'

'Not if I have anything to say about it,' he said angrily.

'Well, fortunately for me, you haven't,' she said shortly, 'so you wasted your time following me here.'

'Following you? What are you talking about?'

She sighed with exaggerated patience. 'To this hospital.'

He laughed. 'And you talk about my ego? I had this job lined up long before I met you, sweetheart.'

'Very convincing—I almost believe you,' she said sweetly, and walked into the interview-room.

'Hello, are you Petra Brown's mother? I'm Maggie Wells, the paediatric SHO. Mrs Brown, I want you to tell me everything you can about the times when Petra's broken something in the past.'

*   *   *

Maggie walked out of Sister's office later that day and bumped straight into Ben. He caught her arm to steady her, and then continued to hold it lightly.

'I was looking for you,' he said.

'I have nothing to say to you,' she told him bluntly. 'Now let me pass, please.' She glared pointedly at his hand, and he released her with a muffled curse.

'It's about Petra,' he told her, his voice harsh, and she sighed tiredly.

'Oh. Sorry. Well, it appears we were right. Michael Barrington, the orthopaedic SR, has had a look at the X-rays and confirmed the diagnosis provisionally, but he wants a full skeletal scan done, and chromosome analysis. She's having a hearing test tomorrow, but I gather she's been regarded as educationally backward at play-group.'

'Why the hell didn't the health visitor pick up the hearing loss?' Ben asked angrily. 'That kind of lapse really is inexcusable.'

'What about all the other fractures? They got through. We're so obsessed with child abuse these days sometimes I think we don't see what's under our noses.'

'But you did—well done.'

She shrugged. 'You would have.'

'I don't know—you got the legionnaires', too. I get the impression you're a pretty good diagnostician, Maggie.'

'You'd thought of that before me,' she pointed out fairly.

'Ah, but I didn't believe it. You back your hunches—I try logic first, and not always successfully.'

She gave him a strained smile. 'Call it women's intuition. Ben, I have to go, I'm needed in SCBU.'

He glanced at his watch. 'Yes, I have to get back to A and E. Look, Maggie, about tonight——'

'No, Ben. Please. Just let it drop.'

His face registered hurt and disappointment for a second before he blanked it out.

'If that's the way you want to play it,' he said shortly.

'It is.'

'Right. I'll see you around.'

He turned on his heel and walked away, and Maggie watched him go, her heart aching. Damn it, why did he have to be here? No wonder Lucinda had been so keen for her to go on the cruise—here in the hospital, with all the competition, she wouldn't have stood a chance. Not that it mattered, anyway, as he was getting married, but that probably wouldn't stop him. She just hoped she didn't keep hearing about all his affairs over the hospital grapevine.

It was a hope that was doomed to failure. Everywhere she went, people were talking about the new A and E senior registrar and his flashy sports car.

Maggie didn't even know he had one, but somehow she wasn't surprised.

Jo and Annie were horrified when she told them Ben was working in the hospital.

'What a ghastly coincidence!' Anne exclaimed.

Maggie snorted. 'Rubbish. Lucinda knew, you can be sure of that. I expect she set us up to give me a head start—after all, there are a lot of pretty women in this hospital. Without a shove to the front I'd be a long way down the queue.'

She ignored Jo and Annie rolling their eyes and groaning.

'Haven't you noticed,' Jo asked her sweetly, 'just how many of the young doctors drool after you?'

'But they're awful!'

'And you're just too fussy.'

'Apparently not,' she commented drily, and, leaving her friends shaking their heads in concern, she returned to the ward and threw herself back into routine.

She went to see her grandmother after work.

'Guess who I ran into today?' she asked without beating around the bush.

'Oh, dear. Was it embarrassing?'

'Embarrassing? You might have told me—honestly, Lucinda, I swear I'll kill you if you interfere in my life again!'

Lucinda laid a soothing hand on her agitated granddaughter's arm and patted gently. 'I'm truly sorry, darling. It's just that Gerald had told me so much about him——'

'Gerald? I *knew* he was involved in this.'

'Oh, yes—he's Ben's stepfather. He adores the boy.'

Maggie fixed her grandmother with a steely eye. 'He is not a boy, Grannie, and I am not a girl. We are adults, both of us, and don't need our lives arranged and set up by a pair of interfering old busybodies!'

She leapt up and paced across the room, knocking her handbag to the floor as she did so. It burst open and the contents spilled out—including the box containing the string of pearls that Lucinda spotted immediately.

'What's in there?' she asked with avid curiosity.

'Pearls—Ben bought them for me.' She laughed as she remembered how he had asked the shop-keeper to find some cheaper ones. 'They're nothing special—they aren't even very well matched.'

She handed the box to her grandmother, and Lucinda opened it and started to chuckle.

'I didn't think they were that awful,' Maggie said defensively.

Her grandmother smiled and stroked the pearls lovingly. 'Darling girl, these are real pearls, horribly expensive and far more valuable than cultured pearls. That's why they aren't perfectly matched. Sweetheart, these pearls are extremely rare and very, very lovely. You should have them valued for insurance.' She shut the box and looked up at her granddaughter. 'You must have meant something very special for him to buy them for you.'

She swallowed hard. 'I did think so, but it seems I was wrong.'

'Tell me.'

Maggie sat down again and took the pearls, run-ning her finger over them in memory.

'Oh, I caught him in a compromising position—and not once, but twice, with two different women,' she explained, recalling the Barbie-doll of New Year's Eve who she had seen coming from the vicinity of Ben's cabin the following morning, still dressed in her party finery. 'He's got the morals of an alley-cat, but he's very convincing.'

'Did he hurt you very badly, darling?' her grand-mother asked gently.

'Yes—yes, he did. Oh, Lucinda, why did you have to do it?'

She snapped the box shut, pushed the pearls back into her bag and stood up.

'Please, I beg of you, don't interfere now. We have to work together—that's going to be hard enough without any further meddling. Just leave us alone.'

She let herself out and drove home, seething still at the knowledge that Gerald was Ben's stepfather. In which case, why didn't Lucinda know that Ben was getting married? Oh, well, she would in time, and then she would be sure to back off. In the meantime Maggie would just give the old girl a wide berth.

The following day she was too busy to think, but on the Wednesday she took a long lunch break and went into town to a jeweller's that specialised in quality gems.

'I wonder if you could value these for me for insurance?' she asked, and handed the box to the assistant.

She went out into the back of the shop and emerged with the owner, a wizened little man with a hunch back and twinkling eyes.

'I understand you would like these valued, is that right?'

Maggie nodded. 'Yes, for insurance.'

He opened the flap in the counter and beckoned for her to follow him.

'Come into my office,' he said, and led her into a stuffy little room with a dark, heavy desk and a huge safe in one corner.

'Now, my dear, do take a seat. Can you tell me where you got them?'

While he was asking questions and Maggie was answering them, he was peering at the pearls under a microscope and shining lights on them, measuring them with dividers and jotting notes on a pad.

Finally he set them down, lifted his glasses off his nose and peered at Maggie over the desk.

'Very nice,' he commented. 'Do you happen to know what they cost in Singapore?'

Maggie shrugged. 'I'm afraid I have no idea—a few hundred pounds, I imagine—he haggled.'

The man smoothed the pearls lovingly with a gnarled fingertip. 'Well, my dear, if your friend only paid a few hundred pounds he secured a real bargain. To replace them in this country, which would be extremely difficult, would cost something in the region of fifteen to twenty thousand pounds.'

Maggie was speechless.

The man suggested putting his valuation in writing for the insurance company, and she nodded numbly, thanked him in a weak voice and left, clutching her bag with the pearls safely stashed inside firmly against her chest.

She made a detour on the way home to the bank, where she put the pearls in a safe deposit box, and returned to the hospital still in a state of shock.

She bumped into Anne Gabriel in the corridor and recounted the story to her, and left her open-mouthed as she went on to the ward.

Little Petra Brown was looking better, her arm comfortable now, and the results of her tests were due that afternoon.

A little after three o'clock Michael Barrington came up and found her.

'Got the results on Petra,' he said. 'Looks like you were right—she's had several fractures and there's evidence of other sorts of skeletal trauma—small crush fractures, that sort of thing, all entirely consistent with osteogenesis imperfecta.'

'What about her hearing?'

'Almost total loss in her left ear, significant impairment in the right. Goodness knows how it escaped detection.' He perched on the edge of the desk and rubbed his left knee gingerly.

'Are you OK?'

He smiled wryly. 'I'll live. The cold seems to play havoc with my stump, and where the strap bears over the top of my patella.'

'Don't you think it would have been better to take it easy and not jump straight back in? You were back to work within weeks of losing your leg—all very admirable, but don't you think you'll pay the price as you get older if you don't ease off now?'

Michael laughed. 'Probably, but I'm not about to try. Life's too short. Did you know Clare and I are planning to sail the Atlantic in *Henrietta* next summer?'

Maggie was amazed, but at the same time not surprised. Michael had shown enormous courage since the accident in which he had lost his leg, and his determination to get back into the mainstream and do at least as much as he had before was a moving example to the amputees in his care.

'How is Clare now?' she asked.

'Oh, fine. That ectopic pregnancy was just one of

those unfortunate things, but I'm waiting now for the third thing to go wrong.'

Maggie laughed and tutted. 'Superstitious, Michael?' she teased.

'Not really. Right, on the subject of Petra, I suppose I'd better see the social workers and the parents and see if we can't sort out these allegations of abuse. Perhaps Peter would like to be in on the meetings?'

Assuring Michael that she would pass on the message, she went up to SCBU and checked over her babies. One or two were giving cause for concern, and she was late going off duty.

On the way out she saw Ben laughingly showing Kathleen Hennessy, the A and E sister, into his car.

It was red and racy, and neither it nor the way he was settling Kathleen surprised Maggie.

She arrived home to her freezing cold flat in a foul mood, and, after a hot bath to soak out the aches and pains, she curled up in front of the fire with a book.

However, it couldn't hold her attention.

She kept seeing Ben and Kathleen laughing together in the car park, and she wondered for the thousandth time since lunch why, when he was so apparently promiscuous, he should have bought her such expensive pearls?

Surely not all his girlfriends were treated in the same way? Heavens, it would cost the man hundreds of thousands a year, and he was only a senior reg!

Perhaps it was only the difficult ones who took too long to succumb to his charm—although God knew she had succumbed quickly enough by anybody's standards!

She abandoned her book and sat staring into the hissing flames of the gas fire, brooding on her doomed relationship with the only man she had ever loved.

The phone started her out of her reverie, and she snatched it up, her voice slightly breathless.

'Hello?'

'Maggie? It's Bron Henderson. Look, we're having a party on Saturday—just a few friends round for drinks to celebrate my retirement from active service, as Oliver puts it. Would you be able to come?'

Caught on the hop, unable to think of a ready excuse, Maggie found herself agreeing.

'Oh, well, perhaps it'll do me good,' she muttered as she prepared for bed. 'I can't sit around and mope forever, and—who knows?—I might meet someone nice to take my mind off him.'

But she knew it was a vain hope. Like her father, she loved once and then it was forever. And like him, she was doomed to a lifetime of sorrow and regret.

CHAPTER SEVEN

MAGGIE'S plan to avoid Ben as far as possible would have been fine if they hadn't had to work together. As it was, every time a child came into A and E needing admission a paediatrician was called, and nine times out of ten it was Maggie.

On Thursday morning she was called to a child of nine who had been ill for a few days and whose mother had been unable to rouse him that morning.

Hurrying down to A and E, she found Ben in the cubicle with the boy and his anxious mother.

'Morning,' Ben said, his voice civil but his eyes unfriendly.

You can't have everything, Maggie told herself firmly, and produced a smile.

'Good morning. Who's this, then?'

'Stephen Phillips, aged nine. This is his mother.'

She acknowledged the mother and turned to the still form of the little boy.

'Any history?' she asked.

'He's been tired and floppy for a few days—he had a cold a week ago, and he hasn't been right since,' the mother said worriedly. 'Then he started being sick, and our GP said he probably had a tummy bug. There's a lot of it at his school at the moment. He's been right off his food—all he'll do is drink, drink, drink. Then last night he could hardly stay awake, and I sent him to bed early, and this morning I couldn't really wake him.'

Maggie nodded, checked his pupils to see if they were even, and ran her hands over the little boy's chest and abdomen. 'He's very thin—has he lost weight?'

'Yes, well, he's grown, and you know how they seem to get so skinny till they fill out again, but this time he hasn't seemed to fill out—rather the contrary.'

Maggie plucked up a fold of papery skin from his tummy and watched as it wrinkled and then stayed pinched up, a sure sign of dehydration.

Frowning, she pulled his lower jaw down and sniffed his breath.

'Ketones,' Ben said from behind her.

'Yes, he's very acetotic, isn't he? Well, Mrs Phillips, we need to run some tests, but the first thing to do is to get some fluid into Stephen and get the balance of his blood chemistry right again.'

Maggie perched on a chair beside the woman and took her hand. 'Mrs Phillips, has anyone in your family or your husband's family got a history of diabetes?'

'Diabetes?' The woman was clearly shocked. 'What—you surely don't think. . .? He can't. . .'

'We have to run a whole series of tests, but at the moment that looks the most likely cause of Stephen's coma. We'll have to admit Stephen now, and hopefully he'll start to pick up again as soon as we get the balance better. We'll need to take some blood for testing, and a urine sample, but we have to move fast. He's very critically ill at the moment.'

'Yes—yes, of course. Do whatever you have to. . .'

They set up an IV line, took blood for analysis

and arranged for his admission. Hopefully if they ran in a quantity of fluid to boost his blood volume, the haemodilution would restore the balance of electrolytes in his blood, and an injection of insulin would help to lower the blood sugar.

Then, and only then, would they see some improvement, but it would take hours rather than minutes, and possibly even days, before they could be confident that he was going to pull through, and then probably weeks until he was stabilised on insulin and able to go home.

While they were working on him the mother was taken to the interview-room and given a cup of tea, and Maggie was left alone with Ben.

'How's Petra?' he asked.

'Better, but the skeletal scan confirmed the diagnosis.'

'Poor kid. Fancy facing a life of broken bones. How's her hearing?'

'Pretty awful—almost total loss in the left ear.' Maggie secured the cannula on the back of Stephen's hand with a wide strip of tape, and adjusted the flow of the drip. 'Her right ear's better, so with a hearing aid she should be able to hear much more clearly than she has been. I expect she'll pick up enormously once that happens.'

She straightened up. 'Right, if we can find a porter we can get this young man up to ITU and settle him in. Thank you, Ben.'

He gave a wry, humourless smile. 'Don't thank me, Maggie—just doing my job.'

She met his eyes and felt the breath go out of her lungs. Why couldn't she manage to hate him? It would make life so much easier.

She turned briskly away and went out into the corridor, hailed a porter and made her way to ITU to brief the staff on Stephen's admission.

Mrs Phillips came up with her son a short while later, and Maggie finished clerking him and then handed over to Peter Travers.

She went back to the ward where another child had dislodged her drip, and by the time she had set up another line she was needed in SCBU.

The morning flew by, and when she went into lunch she found Jo and Alex Carter sitting at a window table, their heads together, laughing softly.

She felt a pang of jealousy and stifled it instantly. What did she have to be jealous of? Jo, unable to have children through a tragic twist of fate; Alex, widowed five years ago and now happy again at last with Jo but having to forsake the possibility of having children of his own because of his commitment to her; and Amy, the child they both desperately wanted to adopt if they could only convince Social Services that it would be best for her. Without the mother's suicide note leaving Amy in Jo's care they wouldn't even have been considered, and even now it was still touch and go.

Did Maggie really envy them all that?

Yes. Because, through it all, they had their love to keep them going.

She picked up a plate of chicken supreme and rice and a cup of coffee and made her way to a table on the other side of the room. She didn't want to intrude on the little time they had together.

Annie joined her a few minutes later.

'It's disgusting the way those two carry on in

public!' she said laughingly. 'Mind if I sit here? I'd feel distinctly *de trop* over there!'

'No, do,' Maggie said with a listless smile. 'How's Beth?'

Annie grinned. 'Oh, little tyke! She's fine. She's seven in a few weeks and wants to join Brownies. I can hardly believe she's so old. It only seems like yesterday. . .'

'It must have been very hard to bring her up on your own.'

'Oh, no, she's been a joy, and my parents were wonderful.'

Maggie fiddled with her food. 'Annie, did you ever consider having a termination?'

Anne's face froze. 'Yes, I thought about it—for about ten seconds, but I couldn't kill his child.'

'You must have loved him very much.'

Anne glanced up, and the raw emotion in her eyes made Maggie reach out and cover her hand in comfort.

'I'm sorry—I didn't mean to pry. It's really none of my business.'

'It's OK. I had a boyfriend at the time—everybody assumed she was his.'

'But?'

'She wasn't. She was the result of one wild, glorious night.'

'With a stranger?' Maggie was surprised.

'Oh, no. J—— He was no stranger. I'd known him for years.'

'And loved him.'

'Yes.' Her voice was a mere thread of sound. 'Yes, I'd loved him.' She sighed shakily.

'Do you ever regret having Beth?'

'Oh, no!' Anne shook her head vehemently. 'Only for her sake, that she hasn't got a father, but there are so many single parents these days that I don't think she even notices most of the time.'

She lapsed into a thoughtful silence, and Maggie ate her lunch mechanically and wondered how she would have felt if she had conceived Ben's child.

She hadn't, she knew that now, but as she considered the idea she felt a sharp pang of loss.

No, Anne would have kept her child, of course, regardless of the difficulties—just as Maggie would have done if fate had given her the opportunity.

Ben, actually, rather than fate, because, despite his other faults, he had been conscientious about that aspect of their relationship, never once taking chances.

She sighed. Really she ought to be glad, but somehow, stupidly, she wasn't.

Her bleep squawked, and she abandoned the rest of her meal almost gratefully and made her way back to the ward.

The rest of the week passed in a blur. Stephen Phillips recovered consciousness late on Friday morning, and once his condition had stabilised would be transferred to the paediatric ward.

Petra Brown had been discharged, and Social Services were already working with the family to try and establish the precise extent of their violence towards the fragile child. Clearly there needed to be changes in the family's attitude—there was no room in Petra's life for the sort of flashfire smacks delivered in anger that most children weathered without harm. She simply wasn't strong enough, and her

family would have to be made aware of that in no
uncertain terms.

She was in the canteen snatching a cup of tea
midway through Friday afternoon when Ben came
up and stood beside her.

'May I join you?'

She closed her eyes. 'If you must.'

He snorted tiredly. 'I don't have to, Maggie. I just
wanted to ask about Stephen Phillips.'

She sighed. Why did he have to be so
conscientious?

'He's doing OK, I think. He's conscious now, and
I expect they'll move him later today. Was that all?'

She met his eyes challengingly, and after a few
seconds he exhaled sharply, and his lips tightened in
irritation. 'Yes, that was all. Have a good weekend.'

He turned on his heel and walked away, and
Maggie picked up her tea with trembling fingers.

'Damn him,' she muttered, and then her fingers
shook more violently and she slopped tea on her
white coat.

'Got the DTs?'

She looked up. 'Oh. Hello, Kathleen.'

'Mind if I join you?' The A and E sister was
already sitting down, propping her feet on another
chair and resting her head back, her eyes closed.

Maggie tried not to hate her for going out with
Ben—if indeed she had been. There was probably
some innocent explanation for her getting into his
car the other night.

'Busy?' she asked, more for conversation than
because she really cared at that moment.

'I should say—and I'm on this weekend. Pity, I
was looking forward to Bron's party.'

'You must miss her,' Maggie said. She had become quite friendly with the A and E registrar over the past eighteen months since she started her house jobs, and she imagined the casualty staff had too.

'Oh, yes, but she was finding her pregnancy quite hard going,' Kathleen was saying. 'I must say it's nice to be able to make Ben run around without a conscience. I used to feel guilty every time I asked Bron to look at anyone, but Ben's always there first. He's an absolute powerhouse—well, you know that, of course. You were on the cruise with him when all those poor people went down with legionnaires'.'

'Yes, he's—er—a very good doctor.'

Kathleen agreed. 'He's marvellous. He's spotted all sorts of things I would have missed, like that child with osteogenesis imperfecta—he took one look at her, apparently, and realised what was wrong.'

Maggie frowned. That wasn't how she remembered it at all! Was he now stooping to claiming her diagnoses as his own?

With a little snort of disgust, she got to her feet. 'Sorry, I'm going to have to leave you, Kath. Duty calls.'

Somehow she got through the rest of the day without going down to A and E and strangling him with her bare hands. How *dared* he tell Kathleen that he had taken one look at Petra and diagnosed her condition? He hadn't had a clue, apart from the obvious possibility of abuse—damn him!

Saturday morning found her still angry, and at a loose end. She rang Jo Carter and asked if she was free.

'Well, ish. Alex is operating and Annie's assisting,

so I've got Beth for the morning, but you're welcome to come round and join us,' she explained.

So Maggie tugged on some jeans and a thick sweater, pushed her feet into warm leather boots and drove over to the Carters' house. As she climbed out of her car, she glanced up at the house and sighed. Jo was very lucky to have met Alex and fallen in love. They had a super house, and a wonderful marriage if they could only find time for it.

She rang the doorbell and listened to the giggles and running footsteps.

'Hello, Auntie Maggie.'

She smiled down at the dark-haired, gappy-toothed child laughing up at her.

'Hello, darling. How are you today?'

'Great—Auntie Jo and I are painting—come and see!'

She grabbed Maggie's hand in her paint-splattered little paw and towed her towards the kitchen.

Jo was perched at the breakfast table, a sea of newspapers and sticky dawbs surrounding her, and a streak of yellow paint adorning her cheek.

'I like the new make-up,' Maggie said with a laugh. 'Very fetching!'

Jo smiled wryly. 'Am I covered? It's not surprising. Drag up a seat if you can find anywhere safe, and I'll make some coffee for you while you tell me all about it.'

And Maggie, who hadn't meant to blab and criticise, found herself telling Jo all about Ben and Petra and what Kathleen had said.

'The ship's rat is flying true to form, then?' Jo said with a touch of sarcasm, and Maggie bit her lips.

Had she really been so wrong about him? What a rotten judge of character she must be.

'Did Annie tell you about the pearls?' she asked suddenly.

'The pearls?'

'Yes—the necklace he gave me.'

'Oh, yes, you mentioned it—no, Annie hasn't said anything to me. . .mind, we've been so busy I've hardly seen her. This cold weather seems to have brought on a spate of deliveries. What about it?'

'I had it valued on Wednesday, for insurance.'

'And?'

'Fifteen to twenty thousand pounds?'

Jo almost dropped her tea in her lap. 'Wha—how——? My God! You jest!'

Maggie shook her head. 'No, I don't. It was my grandmother who made me think—she said they were real and not cultured, and I should have them looked at. I wish I hadn't bothered, because I can't possibly keep them now.'

Jo snorted. 'Why ever not? If he's fool enough to give them to you, you jolly well ought to keep them! But twenty thousand—where did he get that much money?'

'Credit card.'

'Twenty thousand? Some credit card!'

'He didn't pay that much, Jo, I'm sure. He haggled him down, and he seemed to know the old boy—I doubt if he was cheated.'

Jo whistled. 'Even so.'

'Exactly. Now why would he spend so much on me when he's just about to get married? And where did he get it from?'

'Family money?'

Maggie snorted. 'Quite likely—he certainly didn't come by it honestly! No, I shall have to give them back—I wouldn't dare wear the wretched things!'

At that point Beth decided she was bored with painting. 'Can we feed the ducks, Auntie Jo?' she begged.

'OK—but get cleaned up first. Want to come, Maggie? There's a duckpond just up the road opposite the church. It's quite a nice little walk, and you look as if you could do with the fresh air.'

'Why not? It beats sitting at home feeling sorry for myself.' With a self-mocking little laugh, she stood up and started folding up the paint-soaked newspaper.

Maggie dressed carefully for the party that night, as much for bravado as anything.

She piled her hair up on top of her head and teased out the curls so that it fell in a soft mass from the crown, and then in a touch of defiance she changed her lipstick for a more vibrant pink and slipped into her little black dress.

She hadn't had time to have it cleaned since Singapore, and there was a lingering trace of Ben's cologne that drifted from it as she settled it on her shoulders. Stifling the urge to cry, she zipped the back and determinedly got out the fine batik shawl and draped it round her shoulders.

That would do. A quick spritz of perfume and she snuggled into her thick coat and let herself out.

The weather was worsening, so she left in plenty of time and drove carefully to Bron and Oliver's big red-brick house on the park. There was plenty of room on the drive, and she tucked her car into a corner and rang the bell.

Oliver answered the door, his arms full of wriggling child. 'Hi, Maggie, come on in.'

'Hello, Oliver. I'm sorry I'm early, but I wasn't sure how bad the roads would be.'

'That's fine,' he said. 'You can meet Matt and Polly. I'm just trying to persuade my daughter it's time for bed, and then I'll be down. Bron's in the kitchen with the others—go and find her.'

Maggie ruffled the child's blonde curls and winked at her. 'Hello, Livvy. How's my little friend today?'

'OK. I'm having a baby!'

'I know. Will that be lovely?'

'T'riffic! Mummy's going to stay at home now, so I can play with her.'

Maggie smiled. 'You'll enjoy that. Sleep well, poppet,' she said, and made her way into the kitchen.

Bron was there, and a couple Maggie didn't recognise. Bron, decidedly pregnant but still lovely, introduced her, and handed her a glass of mulled wine.

The woman, Polly, was sitting at the table breast-feeding a little baby, and her husband was standing near by, his eyes straying back to his wife and child every few seconds, as if he couldn't quite believe they were there.

'Matt's an old friend of Oliver's from his London days,' Bron explained. 'He's a GP now at Longridge, and Polly's his practice nurse.'

'Was!' Polly corrected laughingly. 'I'm too busy now to be anything but a mum.'

Bron smiled. 'Isn't Alice sweet?'

'Lovely.' Maggie crouched beside Polly and brushed the baby's head lightly. 'What a pretty baby—how old is she?'

'Four and a half months.' The baby's mouth was relaxed now, and Polly eased her off the breast and held her out to Matt.

'May I?' Maggie asked.

'I should think so—can we trust you?' Matt teased.

'I hope so—I'm a paediatrician!'

'Oh—fine! Have her. She'll probably throw up on you.'

Maggie laughed and sat herself down in a chair with a towel on her lap and winded the sleepy infant with practised ease.

Then she snuggled her into the crook of her arm and watched, spellbound, as her little face settled into sleep.

'It's lovely to see a healthy, happy baby,' she said softly.

Matt and Polly laughed. 'She doesn't always look so delightful,' Maggie was assured. 'She's like the girl who had a little curl, right in the middle of her forehead!'

'Oh, for shame,' Maggie protested, 'surely she's never horrid?'

Matt chuckled. 'Only at night, usually the night after I've been on call! Here, let me have the little scamp. I'll change her and put her down. Which room are we putting her in, Bron?'

'Oh, the one next to Livvy—Maggie, I wonder if you'd be a dear and put the nibbles out in the drawing-room? I still haven't got round to it.'

While they put the baby down and Polly tidied

herself up in the cloakroom, Maggie set out the nibbles and tidied up in the kitchen.

She was just finishing when the doorbell rang.

'Maggie, would you get it?' Bron called.

'You need a maid!' she called back laughingly, and opened the front door.

'Ben——!'

'Hello, Maggie.'

He was the last person she had expected to see, and she stood rooted to the spot, her heart pounding. 'What are you doing here?' she managed, rather stupidly.

'I've been invited to a party, the same as you, I imagine.'

She remained there, unable to move, cursing herself for the lack of foresight that might have predicted his presence. After all, he had taken over from Bron. . .

'Are you going to let me in, or are you going to stand there all night while all the heat pours out of the front door and I freeze to death on the step?'

Belatedly she collected herself and stepped back. 'No—I—come in. I'm sorry. I just wasn't expecting it to be you.'

His face twisted into a wry grin. 'I'm sorry it was such an unpleasant shock. Perhaps it will give us a chance to rekindle the flame.'

'No! Ben, please. . .'

'Oh, forget it—hi, Oliver!'

'Ben! Welcome to the madhouse. Come on in, let me take your coat. Do you know Maggie Wells?'

He met Maggie's eyes and his were touched with a rueful humour. 'Yes, we have met.'

Maggie faded out of the way while Oliver took

Ben through to the kitchen and offered him a drink, and then Polly emerged from the cloakroom, Matt and Bron came downstairs and the doorbell rang again.

After that it was quite easy to avoid him until she could decently make an early get-away. At ten-thirty she slipped out of the side door, and groaned. Her car, so neatly tucked out of the way, was well and truly blocked in, and it was now bitterly cold—far too cold to walk!

She resigned herself to another hour at least of dodging Ben from room to room, and found a tray of chicken and mushroom vol-au-vents in the kitchen which were quite delicious.

She ate two, and had picked up a third when Ben's voice startled her into dropping it.

'Remember Singapore!' he cautioned in her ear, and then tutted as she dropped the gooey concoction down the front of her black dress.

'Now look what you've done!' she wailed, and he turned her round and dabbed at the mark with his snow-white handkerchief before retrieving the remains from the floor and giving the tiles a wipe.

'What a mucky little thing you are,' he said affectionately, and she didn't know whether to cry or hit him.

'Dance with me,' he murmured, and before she could make up her mind which course of action to take she was in his arms and swaying gently to the music.

His cologne was the same, and the subtle scent brought back so many memories.

Unbidden, her hands crept up and wound round his waist, and he eased her closer, his familiar body aligning itself naturally to hers. It just seemed so right. . .

She felt the tears welling in her eyes, and eased away from him reluctantly.

He let her go—to arm's length, and then held her there, one finger tracing the line of her throat as his eyes met hers hungrily.

'Where are your pearls?' he asked, his voice husky.

She swallowed. 'In the bank, in a safe deposit box—Ben, I had them valued.'

'Oh.'

'Yes, oh. The man told me they would cost between fifteen and twenty thousand to replace.'

'Really? How interesting. I hope they're insured.'

She moved away from him, unable to continue the conversation while his finger trailed enticingly up and down her throat. She might be cross with him, but her body evidently wasn't!

'Of course they're not insured! What did you pay for them?'

He tutted. 'You shouldn't ask—it's not considered polite——'

'I wasn't trying to be polite! Ben, you must realise I couldn't accept them! They're the sort of present you give a—a wife! Anyway, you must have them back.'

'No.'

She sighed and ran her hand through her hair before she remembered it was up. 'Damn.' She skewered the pins back in and glared at him. 'Ben, you have to take them back. Give them to someone else—someone who deserves them.'

His face changed, becoming serious. 'I thought

you did,' he told her gently. 'I couldn't think of anyone who deserved them more.'

She snorted inelegantly so she didn't cry. 'Rubbish, Ben. If you won't take them back, I'll just have to pay you for them——'

He laughed, a short, humourless, cold sound that sent a chill over her. 'You already have, if you remember. I took my payment in kind.'

The words cut her to the quick. How could he talk about the most wonderful thing that had ever happened to her in such mercenary and damning tones? 'That's a terrible thing to say!' she whispered.

'But we agreed—don't you recall? It was in Singapore. You said it would take a lifetime, but in view of the fact that you so generously gave me your virginity, I'm prepared to overlook the next fifty years——'

He was quick, but she got there first, the flat of her hand connecting savagely with his cheek.

Then she turned on her heel and stalked out, snatching a full glass of wine off the side as she passed.

The party was in full swing, and Maggie plastered on her brave face and threw herself into it with gusto.

Mick O'Shea, one of the other house doctors who had started at the same time as her, detached himself from the wall and moved towards her.

'Dance, Maggie?' he asked.

Out of the corner of her eye she saw Ben follow her into the room, and she agreed cheerfully, really letting herself go.

After two fast numbers the music slowed, and Mick held out his arms.

Ben was leaning against the wall, watching her with an enigmatic and unreadable expression on his face, and she went into Mick's arms with a warmer smile than her feelings for him warranted.

As the evening wore on, she drank more and more wine, flirted outrageously with all the men—married and single—and behaved more and more affectionately towards poor Mick until Ben pulled her aside, his eyes flashing angrily.

'For God's sake, woman, he's going to blow a fuse in a minute!' he muttered furiously. 'Either take him up to bed or leave him alone, but stop wriggling against him like a frustrated snake!'

Maggie swung her hand up, but this time he was ready for her.

'I think you've had enough. I'm going to take you home before you offend these good people.'

'I'm not going anywhere with you!' she told him loudly. 'And anyway, I can't go home, my car's blocked in!'

'You aren't driving anywhere for at least the next twelve hours!'

She snatched her arm away from him. 'You want a bet?'

She pushed past him and made her way rather unsteadily to the side hall where the coats were hanging.

'I mean it,' he said, following her.

'Get lost.'

She found her coat and pulled it on, buttoned it more or less and picked up her bag.

Oliver was standing behind Ben.

'Thank you for a lovely party,' she said as precisely as she could manage.

Oliver closed his eyes for a second and sighed.

'Don't worry, I'll look after her,' Ben assured him.

'I don't need looking after!' Maggie protested, and could have screamed when her efforts failed to open the door.

'Allow me,' Ben said politely, and turned the handle.

Of course—how silly of me, she thought blearily. Now, where's the car?

But the keys wouldn't play ball.

'I appear to need your help after all—would you open my car for me?' she asked, handing him the keys.

He pocketed them with a deadpan expression.

'What the hell are you doing? I asked you to help me!'

'And that's exactly what I am doing,' he replied. 'You're still blocked in. I'll give you a lift, and you can come back tomorrow and collect it.'

'No.'

'Yes.' He hooked his arm through hers and led her, protesting all the way, to his car, then he fed her into the passenger-seat, slammed the door and ran round to the driver's side while she was still fumbling for the catch.

She was about to climb out again as he swung himself into his seat and hauled her back, fastened her seatbelt and clamping her hands in one of his.

'Just to make sure you don't do anything silly,' he said, and drove one-handed back to her flat.

'You're a pig,' she said flatly. 'I hate you.'

'Fine.'

'I do—and I'm going to report you for driving one-handed!'

'Good job it's an automatic,' he commented, and released her.

The cold air was beginning to have the most strange effect on her. She felt positively dizzy as she climbed out of the car and had to wait for Ben to help her up the stairs.

He took her into her flat, led her to her bedroom and stripped off her dress.

'That takes a lot of practice,' she announced seriously as he dealt with her uncooperative arms.

'I've put a lot of drunks to bed in my time,' he told her.

'I am not drunk!' she answered belligerently.

'Of course not—arms up!'

She obeyed, sat heavily on the bed and glared at him.

'Why are you undressing me?'

'Because you're going to bed.'

She crossed her arms defensively. 'Not with you, you philanderer! You needn't think you're going to stay the night!'

He gave a derisive snort. 'Perish the thought!' he said. 'Consider the debt paid on the pearls, Maggie. I'd hate to end up beholden to you.'

And he turned on his heel and left her, sitting almost naked in her freezing-cold bedroom, staring after him.

'I know,' she said to the empty room. 'I've decided what to do—I'll cry.'

But she couldn't remember how to, not for hours, and then she couldn't remember how to stop.

CHAPTER EIGHT

MAGGIE didn't enjoy Sunday. She finally woke around noon, with a pounding head and a raging thirst, and gulped down a tumbler of cold water and some aspirin, which she promptly lost.

Miserable, she crawled back to bed, confident in the knowledge that she would never make an alcoholic.

As the long and awful day wore on, so more and more of the previous night's events returned to her, and the hangover she had woken with was replaced by a gut-wrenching misery.

Not only was she totally humiliated by her own behaviour, there was also Ben's to consider, and the awful things he had said to her were burned forever into her heart.

She dreaded seeing him again, although one thing was now painfully clear: if he wouldn't take back the pearls, she would sell them and donate the money to charity—perhaps AIDS research, an area that Jo Carter was getting heavily involved with these days.

After all, he had made it bitingly clear that he considered she had earned them, so she might as well dispose of them as she saw fit.

But not today. Today, she thought, I will lie here and wallow in self-pity, and wonder how on earth I will face all my colleagues in the morning. Perhaps I'll ring in sick?

But she knew she wouldn't.

Monday morning was cold, bright, and brought the miserable realisation that she hadn't collected her car from the Hendersons' after Saturday night and so had no way of getting back to work.

God is on my side after all, she thought with a wry attempt at humour, and then, as she was walking down the path in time to catch the bus, she saw the car neatly parked in the road outside her flat.

Ben must have returned it—though God knew why after the way they had spoken to each other.

She parked at the hospital and went in through the side door in the maternity wing and up to SCBU, the place where she was least likely to bump into anyone who had witnessed her disgrace.

There a baby with hydrocephalus had been born over the weekend, and had had a shunt installed, a fine tube that drained the excess fluid from around the brain into the abdominal cavity to prevent brain damage from the build-up of pressure within the skull.

She checked his condition, and the intra-cranial pressure, and then examined one or two of the other babies the nursing staff were concerned about.

So far so good.

Then an unavoidable call, to the ward, took her out into the main body of the hospital.

She passed an unbelievable number of people, many of whom smiled and said hello quite normally, but there were others who smiled knowingly and said hello in quite a different tone, and by the time she reached the relative sanctuary of the ward she was ready to crawl into a corner and hide for a few years.

She checked the child she had been called to look

at, another weekend admission, and then chatted to some of the others to see how they were doing. They, at least, hadn't witnessed her humiliation.

Stephen Phillips was making steady progress, and his mother was gradually coming to terms with the shock of his diabetes. It would be some time before he was stable enough to go home, but he seemed to be enjoying his stay in hospital by all accounts.

She was just going to return to SCBU when she was halted by the urgent summons of her bleep.

Going to the ward office, she rang the switchboard, to be told that she was needed in A and E immediately for an extremely urgent admission.

Her heart quailed. She had so wanted to put off this moment, but now she would have to face him. Perhaps they'd be too busy to worry about her appalling behaviour and his blistering sarcasm?

She all but ran down, and found Ben in a cubicle with a distraught young woman and her little boy, who was sitting on her knee fighting noisily for breath. He was cyanosed, the blue line round his mouth a testament to his breathing difficulties, and there was saliva running down his chin.

'Hello, Maggie,' Ben said without a smile. 'This is David Wise. He's feverish, he can't swallow, and I think we need to get him in and intubate him PDQ.'

She nodded, taking in his condition at a glance.

'Epiglottitis?' she said quietly, and he nodded.

'We have to assume so. I've called the senior anaesthetist, the ENT consultant and Peter Travers, and they're all on their way. The theatres are all busy so we'll have to use Resus., but we can't afford to muck about.'

'I can't understand why he can't swallow,' the

mother was saying. 'I can't see anything in his throat—David, open your mouth——'

'No!' they both said at once, but she had seized the little boy's chin and pulled it down, tipping his head back to the light.

Immediately his throat went into spasm, and he started to flail his arms and legs, quite unable to breathe.

Ben snatched the child from his horrified mother, ran across the corridor yelling for the emergency team and dumped him unceremoniously on the trolley.

Maggie, knowing what he was going to do, grabbed David's flailing hands and held them tight.

'It's all right, darling, you'll be all right. We'll get a tube in and you'll be able to breathe again.'

Ben slopped antiseptic over the boy's throat, ordered Kathleen, who had just arrived, to tip back his head and hold it tight, and with a scalpel made a hasty but well-judged incision into the boy's windpipe.

Immediately he began to breathe again, great sobbing lungfuls of air, and the blue line around his mouth started to fade.

'Thank God,' Ben whispered, and Maggie noticed his hands were shaking. 'OK, David,' he said more steadily and with a reassuring smile. 'You'll be all right now. Sorry, old man, that must have been horrid.'

Just then the doors burst open and the ENT consultant, the anaesthetist and Peter Travers came in together.

Ben gave a rueful chuckle. 'Ah, the cavalry,' he murmured. 'Gentlemen, your patient. Kathleen, perhaps it would be an idea to get the mother to sign a consent form?'

There was a ripple of laughter, a mutual relieving of tension, and then the three consultants moved in and took over.

Within moments he was anaesthetised, the incision enlarged and a tracheostomy tube installed, and he was put on intravenous ampicillin to combat the infection.

Maggie, no longer needed, made her escape to the corridor, but then Mick O'Shea waylaid her at the exit from A and E.

'Maggie, are you all right?' he asked without preamble.

She forced a smile. 'Of course—why shouldn't I be?'

He shrugged. 'I just had the feeling that you and Ben Bradshaw had something going—the way he was watching you, and you carrying on as if you were trying to spite him, and him there with a handprint about the size of yours on the side of his face——'

Maggie closed her eyes and sighed. 'We did have something going, Mick, but it's over. I'm sorry I involved you—I wasn't very kind.'

'Oh, think nothing of it!' he chuckled. 'I enjoyed myself, and I know fine well you're not the slightest bit interested in me really. But listen, if I can help— old friends, and all that.'

She was touched. 'Thanks, Mick.' She reached up and kissed his cheek. 'You're a good man—bless you.'

He winked at her and wandered off, hands in his pockets, whistling softly.

'Very touching,' came a quiet voice behind her, and she spun round, her hand over her heart.

'Ben! Good grief, what are you trying to do to me?'

He snorted. 'I thought we'd been over that ground before.'

She flushed to the roots of her hair, and, turning round, she marched up the corridor away from him.

Aggravatingly he fell into step beside her. 'Sorry,' he said, 'that was unfair—and so were a lot of the things I said to you on Saturday.'

She stopped her headlong flight up the corridor, and turned to face him, reluctantly meeting his eyes.

'You were very cruel—it wasn't necessary.'

'I know—I'm sorry.'

'I'm sorry, too. I said some pretty awful things, and my behaviour was outrageous.' She flushed again remembering, and he smiled ruefully.

'Yes, it was, wasn't it? I think my cheek's still bruised, but it looks as if O'Shea's forgiven you.'

'Mick? He's an old friend. He knows it didn't mean anything.'

'I didn't—I was as jealous as hell.'

'You were meant to be. I'm sorry for that, too. It was very childish.'

He held out his hand. 'Truce?' he said softly.

She placed her hand in his, and felt the firm pressure of his grip like an old friend. 'Truce,' she agreed.

His face relaxed into a smile. 'How about a coffee?'

'Good idea, I could do with one after that little lot—you were pretty quick back there with young David.'

He shook his head. 'Don't! I've always dreaded seeing epiglottitis, and the first time I do, hey presto! I'm just glad I missed the jugular!'

She laughed, and together they walked up to the canteen, more natural with each other than they had been in the whole of the previous week.

On the way in they bumped into Jo and Annie who were just leaving, and Maggie was horribly conscious of their thinly disguised astonishment.

'Friends of yours?' Ben asked, and she nodded.

'They're in Obs and Gynae, so I get called in quite a lot by them.'

They collected their coffee and found a spare seat by the window. Maggie was terribly conscious of Ben, and when she glanced up and found his eyes on her, that enigmatic expression in them, she felt a flush creep up on her again.

'Thank you for returning my car,' she said stiffly, to break the ice.

'My pleasure. I had trouble starting it—you should get it looked at. One day it'll let you down.'

She laughed. 'It won't be the first time. It's getting old.'

She thought of his extravagance with the pearls. Now a car, that would have been far more useful, but not nearly as romantic, besides being thoroughly awkward to wear round the neck!

She stirred her coffee absentmindedly, unaware of the slightly rueful smile that played around her lips.

'So,' she said at last, breaking the spell, 'what will happen to little David Wise now?'

Ben leant back in his chair and pulled a face. 'Depends on his recovery. He should be better within a very few days, and hopefully they'll get the tracheostomy tube out by Friday or so. His mother will be looping the loop—I hope she doesn't think she caused that little crisis!'

'But she did!'

He grinned. 'I know that, and you know that, but she doesn't have to, and it could have happened anyway. No, he'll be fine once the swelling's gone down in his throat and he can breathe again without help. How's Stephen Phillips doing?'

They chatted about the patients they had in common, and Ben told her he had heard from Mrs Davis, one of the patients with legionnaires' who they had left in Singapore. She was apparently making good progress, and sent her love to Maggie.

They parted with a friendly smile, and for the first time since her return from the Far East Maggie began to feel that there was light at the end of the tunnel.

True, it hurt in a way to see him, but better that than never to see him again, and so long as they could keep the conversation neutral it seemed they would be able to continue working together—at least until her year as an SHO was up in July. Then, presumably, she would have to look elsewhere for a job as a registrar, by which time she might have got her feelings for Ben into perspective. There was no doubt about it, his wedding in less than three weeks would also help to crystallise her feelings.

A shaft of pain darted through her at the thought, and she threw herself into her work.

David Wise settled over the next few days, and by the end of the week he was able to breath without the tracheostomy tube. The wound was covered and left to heal, and his mother spent a great deal of

time with him. Because of the highly infectious
nature of the *Haemophilus influenzae* bacterium
David was being nursed in isolation, and once the
tube was out he turned into a regular chatterbox.

Ben, of course, popped up every now and again
to see David, and sometimes Maggie would bump
into him there. Between the ward, A and E and the
canteen, she saw him again many times during the
course of the week, and each time they smiled and
stopped for a few words.

It wasn't so much a breach in her defences as a
tentative lowering of guns, but as the days went by
and he made no move to re-establish their previous
relationship she began to relax with him.

And then her car wouldn't start.

It was Monday evening, she had been on call all
weekend, and the three days of sitting in the late
January weather had given the wretched thing the
kiss of death.

Frustrated, light-headed with tiredness and suffer-
ing from an over-exposure to Ben during the weekend, she got out, slammed the door and kicked it.

'Oops.'

She spun round.

'Will you stop creeping up on me?' she snapped.

Ben stifled a smile. 'I didn't need to creep up on
you—you were yelling your head off. I take it you
have problems?'

She snorted. 'Damn thing—what a day to choose!'

'I'm sure it wasn't a personal thing,' he said
rationally.

She debated kicking him, and thought better of it.
He could give her a lift home instead.

She glanced pointedly at his car, parked three spaces up.

His mouth twitched. 'Could I give you a lift home?'

She controlled her smile with difficulty. 'Would you? How kind.'

'Milk of human kindness, me. Hop in.'

He opened the door for her, settled her solicitously into the seat and then slid in behind the wheel.

Laying his hand along the back of her seat, he turned to look behind him while he reversed out of the space and then paused, his hand still unnervingly near her shoulder.

'How about something to eat on the way home?'

She yawned.

'Was that yes or no?' he asked politely.

She giggled, too tired to care. 'Yes, I think— something quick and simple.'

'Italian?'

'Fine.'

They headed into town and he parked the car near a little wine-bar in one of the lanes off the town centre.

It was the sort of place where people often met after work for a glass of wine and a chat, and the atmosphere was relaxed and friendly.

They were shown to a table for two in the corner, and as Ben sat down his knee brushed Maggie's.

The wine-bar, the music, suddenly everything seemed far too intimate, too reminiscent of their time together on the *Island Pearl*.

She shifted discreetly, and toyed with her glass.

Ben, however, seemed totally unmoved. He passed her the menu, told her he was having the

tagliatelle Neapolitan, and then started to discuss
the patients they had dealt with over the weekend.

Reassured by his friendly manner, she relaxed
again and allowed herself to mellow as they ate their
meal and the conversation ebbed and flowed.

Then, in a lull in the conversation, she asked him
about the court case that had driven him away from
England.

'Oh, that.' He paused, looking thoughful, and
swirled the wine in his glass. 'He was only sixty-two,
he had an existing heart condition and he didn't
want to be an invalid. He was a former Olympic
athlete, apparently, and couldn't stand the confines
of his condition.

'He collapsed in the street, and someone called an
ambulance. When they arrived in A and E, the
daughter, who was with him, told me that he had
made one of these living will things, saying that he
didn't want to be kept alive or resuscitated.'

Ben shrugged. 'What could I do? I hadn't seen the
document, I only had her word for it, and for all I
knew she could have had her reasons for wanting
him to die.'

Maggie frowned. 'So why did she call an
ambulance?'

'I don't think she did, but anyway, as she said, she
could hardly let him lie there in the street until he
died, could she?'

'So what happened?'

Ben sighed. 'He arrested, and I resuscitated him
while someone kept the daughter out of the room
and tried to stop her yelling. When he came round
in ITU, he demanded that they disconnect the tubes,

and called his solicitor when they made him sign a disclaimer.

'Somehow he survived, and such was his gratitude he took me to court for saving his life. He died of a massive heart attack two days after they exonerated me for my part in the mess.'

Maggie reached out and took his hand. 'You had no choice, Ben.'

He turned his hand over and squeezed hers affectionately. 'I know, but at the time I felt very confused about my role. Every time anyone arrested I found myself questioning their quality of life and trying to weigh up the validity of resuscitation. In the end someone died while I vacillated, and, although the post mortem proved that he would have died no matter what, I knew it was time to get out and re-evaluate where I was unlikely to do any harm.'

She remembered his hesitation with Vic Matthews in the ship. 'So you escaped to sea?'

He laughed briefly. 'Like joining the Foreign Legion. I knew there was a temporary vacancy coming up on the *Island Pearl*, and it seemed like a good idea. Gerald persuaded me to go, and when Bron announced that she was pregnant and would be leaving permanently he rang me and told me the job was up for grabs.'

She was puzzled. 'How did Gerald know?'

'He lives next door—so do I. I've got a flat in the top of the house.'

She was puzzled. 'But your car was in their drive after the party. . .'

'No, it wasn't. It was next door.'

'I don't remember.'

His mouth quirked. 'I can't say I'm surprised. You were too busy fighting with me to notice where I took you, frankly.'

She flushed and retrieved her hand from his. 'You were very domineering.'

He chuckled. 'Maggie, someone had to be. You would have done yourself a real mischief if you'd managed to get your car out—come on, you know I'm right.'

'I hate people who are always right,' she said huffily, and ruined the effect with a yawn.

'Bed,' he told her, and called for the waiter.

Fifteen minutes later he pulled up outside her flat and stopped the engine, turning to look at her in the dim glow of the street lamps.

'Any chance of a coffee?'

She chewed her lip doubtfully. Was it wise? And yet he'd made it quite clear he had no urge to sleep with her again.

'Quick one,' she replied, and led him up to her little flat.

As the door closed behind them, she was suddenly conscious of the lateness of the hour, his nearness and the very intimate nature of their past.

She slipped off her coat and went into the kitchen, filling the kettle at the sink. She plugged it in and found two clean mugs in the cupboard, and spooned coffee into them with shaking fingers.

'Sorry, the kitchen's a bit of a mess. I didn't have time to clear up on Friday morning——'

'It's fine, Maggie.'

She jumped slightly and scattered coffee granules on the worktop.

'Damn, now look——'

'Forget it,' he said softly. He was standing so close behind her that she could smell the faint trace of his aftershave, and when he reached out his hand and touched her cheek it seemed so natural to turn into his arms, to slide her hands round his waist under his jacket and feel the heat of his skin through the fine cotton of his shirt, to lift her face to his and offer him her lips.

He groaned softly as he took her mouth, his arms lifting her against him so she could feel the immediate response of his body hard against her. It was a passionate kiss, and it was beyond her to protest as his hand slipped beneath the hem of her cotton sweater and found the soft fullness of her breast.

She gave a soft cry and arched against him, and then she was in his arms and he was laying her gently on the bed, his weight pressing her into the mattress, his lips and hands tormenting her as he eased her clothes away and covered her body with his.

He was still dressed, but the fine wool of his trousers left little to the imagination.

She began to shake, her fingers trembling on the buttons of his shirt, and he helped her remove it, coming back to graze her nipples with the coarse texture of his hair-roughened chest.

'Ben!' she sobbed, and his mouth took hers in a wild kiss that drained the last of her fragile resistance.

Then the last scraps of clothing were gone and he was moving over her, joining their bodies with one swift, urgent stroke that sent Maggie crashing over the brink.

Seconds later he joined her, his voice a hoarse shout of triumph as his body shuddered against her.

She lay motionless beneath his weight, feeling the wild pounding of his heart against her breastbone, and a great wave of self-hatred and remorse washed over her at her weakness.

He belonged to another woman, he wasn't hers to hold and to love. In twelve days' time he would be married! How could she have been so weak and so foolish?

He lifted his head and smoothed the hair from her brow. 'All right, my darling?'

She met his eyes, softened with the aftermath of passion, and her own flooded with tears.

'Why did you do that?' she asked, her voice a mere thread of anguish. 'I thought you said the debt was paid?'

Shock flashed in his eyes. 'Maggie, for God's sake. . .'

She turned her head away so that she didn't have to see the bewilderment on his face.

'Please go,' she whispered, and with a muttered curse he rolled away from her and got off the bed. She could hear him fumbling with his clothes, and then after a moment the door closed quietly behind him.

Her heart breaking, she turned her face into the pillow and wept.

CHAPTER NINE

DESPITE her misery Maggie slept, the exhaustion of the weekend mercifully taking her to oblivion.

Not for long enough, though. She knew she would have to face Ben, and when the morning came she rose early, bathed and washed her hair and applied a little make-up to cover the ravages of the night.

The bus was late, and she arrived flustered to find the department in uproar. Drips and drains had worked loose, babies had spiked temperatures for no good reason and the new admissions were tearful and unhappy.

She was quickly swept into the routine, and gradually everything settled down again. Amazingly there were no calls from A and E, and so she was able to avoid Ben for the remainder of the day.

Jo and Annie were less easily avoided.

'What the hell happened to you? You look as if you've been up half the night with Casanova,' Jo said bluntly.

'Jo!' Annie tutted, but Maggie smiled wearily at them.

'Oh, leave her be. She's right—I look a mess.'

'Ben?' Annie asked quietly, and Maggie nodded miserably.

'He gave me a lift home because my car wouldn't start, and he asked himself in for coffee. I should have said no, I should have known what would happen——'

155

She broke off, unable to continue, and Annie made comforting noises while Jo fetched their drinks.

'What is this, tea and sympathy?' she asked with a weak attempt at humour, and they laughed ruefully.

'Poor love,' Jo said gently. 'Really, I could hit him. Some men are just so weak.'

'What about me? You can't blame him for taking what was offered, and, after all, he isn't actually married yet,' Maggie said with typical honesty.

'When's the wedding?' Annie asked.

'Saturday week—eleven days.'

'Damn,' Jo muttered. 'We're going away that day—I've actually managed to persuade Alex we need a holiday.'

'Who's covering?' Annie asked.

'Oh, one of the other consultants said he'll keep an eye, and we're rescheduling some of the less urgent cases. I think we may have found someone to cover me, anyway, but I'd better not say too much or it won't happen! Anyway, as I was saying, we'll be away, but you'll be here, won't you, Annie?'

'I'm on call, I think—especially if you've both abandoned the department!'

Maggie shrugged. 'It's OK. I'll go shopping in Norwich and spoil myself!'

Her bleep called her away then, and she left them shaking their heads worriedly over her.

It was the following morning before she was called down to A and E again, for a baby who had been given a bottle of milk heated in the microwave. Her throat was severely burned, and swelling rapidly.

The mother was almost beside herself with worry

and remorse because she hadn't tested the temperature of the milk, and Maggie was so busy calming her and helping Ben set up an IV line that she didn't have time to worry about the set lines of his face or the way he watched her every move.

Finally the baby was intubated and removed to SCBU, and Ben took Maggie aside.

'Maggie, we have to talk,' he said quietly.

'There's nothing to say, Ben.'

He exhaled sharply. 'How can you say that? Hell, Maggie, we had something really good going for us——'

'Hot sex,' she told him bluntly. 'That's what we had, Ben, that and nothing else. I need more than that from a relationship, but that's all we can ever have, and I'm afraid it's just not enough for me.'

'We have more than that, Maggie, far more! Think back to Penang, to the things we said and did. You can't dismiss it——'

'Ben, you're a very attractive man, and we had an intensely physical interlude——'

'Interlude!'

'It was—that's all it was, Ben, truly.'

His eyes, those lovely grey-blue eyes, searched her face as if he was looking for the truth.

'After all we went through together—can you honestly say you don't love me?' he asked softly.

She sighed raggedly. 'Yes, Ben, I can. I don't love you,' she lied, and then went on more truthfully, 'I can never love you. . .'

Pain flickered in his eyes, and he stepped back away from her.

'Then I apologise for—for what happened the

other night. I didn't mean to force my attentions on
you. I'm sorry.'

'I'm sorry too, Ben. I wish things could have been
different.'

'So do I, Maggie—God, so do I.'

He turned on his heel and walked away, slapping
open a swinging door with the flat of his hand and
walking away from her, his footsteps ringing in the
quiet corridor.

She watched him through the glass pane until he
turned the corner, then with a great sigh she
returned to SCBU and the baby with the burned
throat.

It was a difficult week. Every time she was called
down to A and E or Ben came up to the ward to
follow up on one of his patients, they were civil of
necessity, but he had stopped smiling at her, and in
fact only seemed to smile for the children now.

She knew how he felt. How could she smile at him
when her heart was breaking?

Although, God knew, his heart shouldn't be
breaking. He was getting married in little over a
week—a fact that never left her mind for so much
as a second.

It was on Friday that he finally cornered her in the
quiet of SCBU, while she checked the condition of
the baby with the scalded throat.

'About Monday night,' he said without preamble.

'I don't want to talk about it,' she told him flatly.

'We have to—Maggie, I didn't—in the heat of the
moment I forgot about——' He sighed and ran his
hand through his hair. 'Maggie, you could be
pregnant.'

It had already occurred to her, but she knew that likelihood was extremely remote as her period was due in just two days.

She didn't share that with him, though. Once she might have done, but now, ridiculously, it seemed too personal, altogether too private a thing to tell him.

Instead she laughed softly. 'I'm actually far more concerned with the possibility that having unprotected intercourse with you may have given me AIDS.'

He breathed in sharply. 'Dear God, what must you think of me?'

'I don't know, Ben—you tell me. How the hell do I know how many women you've slept with indiscriminately, or how often? At least you can be sure I haven't given it to you.'

'You're safe, Maggie,' he said, his voice bitter. 'There's no way I'd do that to you—or to myself.'

'Not even in the heat of the moment?' she asked, her voice saccharine-sweet.

'For heaven's sake, Maggie, how promiscuous do you think I am?'

'You don't need to be promiscuous,' she reminded him pointedly. 'Just unlucky—and irresponsible.'

He looked away. 'OK, so I was irresponsible——'

'So was I. It takes two to tango.'

'Just shut up and let me say what I have to say, will you?'

She whirled on him, her eyes flashing. 'What *are* you saying, Ben? Surely you're not going to offer to marry me, are you?'

She turned away before she could see the expression on his face.

'I tell you what, if I am pregnant, I'll use the pearls in lieu of maintenance, OK? Now, if you'll excuse me, I must get on.' She picked up the chart from the end of the cot.

She didn't hear him go, but he must have gone, because when she turned round some time later he was no longer there and the tension drained from her, leaving her empty inside.

The weekend was quiet, enlivened very slightly by a visit to the garage who were trying to resuscitate her car.

'Any joy?' she asked.

'Well,' the man said, scratching his head with an oily finger. 'You need a new set of plug leads and a damned good service, really.'

'Is that cheaper than a new car?'

He laughed. 'A bit.'

'Do it—when can I collect it?'

'Monday afternoon, five o'clock?'

She thanked him, and, as it was a fairly pleasant day, she walked up through the town to the park.

She was on autopilot, really, and was almost surprised to find herself standing staring through the trees and across the road at the Hendersons' house opposite.

Ben lived, of course, on one side or the other. Her eyes scanned the windows, but as it wasn't dark it was difficult to see if anyone was there.

Suddenly conscious of the fact that she was loitering and that someone inside could equally well be watching her, she was just turning to go when Ben's car pulled up and swept on to the drive of the house on the left.

He got out, and then the passenger door opened and Maggie felt her heart sink as his fiancée unfolded herself and rose elegantly to her feet.

'What about the shopping?' Jan said, her voice carrying clearly on the crisp winter air.

'I'll get it later,' Ben replied. 'Come on, let's get warm by the fire.'

He draped an arm casually round the woman's shoulders, and led her into the house. Maggie, stunned with misery, turned and walked aimlessly down through the park, pausing to watch the children feeding the ducks at the pond.

It was possible, of course, that she could be doing that in a couple of years' time with a baby of her own. How would she feel? Would she have Anne Gabriel's courage and determination?

'Please, God, don't let me be pregnant,' she prayed, and then promptly contradicted herself.

In the distance she saw Bron standing by the duckpond with Livvy, but she felt that she really couldn't face talking to her at the moment.

She turned aside and went up another path and back to town via the arboretum, finally arriving home exhausted as dusk settled over the streets.

That evening her grandmother rang.

'Margaret, darling, are you avoiding me?'

'It would serve you right if I was, but actually no, I've just been terribly busy. Are you all right?'

'Oh, yes, darling, you know me, never a day's illness in my life—well, except for a little touch of flu around Christmas,' she added hastily.

Maggie smiled half-heartedly. 'Of course,' she agreed with only a touch of sarcasm.

'So how are things? I gather you've been seeing quite a bit of Ben at work.'

'You could say so.'

Her grandmother sighed. 'Oh, darling, I'm sorry if I've made things difficult for you.'

'Oh, it's not your fault really,' Maggie said, trying to be fair. 'You simply threw us together. Fate did the rest.'

'That's as may be, but I'm still very sorry I interfered and caused you all this distress.'

'Oh, I shall be fine,' Maggie dismissed. 'I'm going to Norwich next Saturday to blow the rest of my holiday money. Do you want to come?'

'Saturday? No, darling, I can't—I'll be going to the wedding.'

'The wedding?' Maggie said stupidly.

'Yes—Jan and——'

'I know. Why are you going?'

'Well—Gerald asked me to. He asked if you would like to come as well, but I wasn't sure, in view of the way you feel about Ben, if——'

'No, Lucinda, I couldn't! I couldn't bear to see him. . .' Married. To see him marrying that lovely girl and promising to be faithful—no, dear God, no!

'Lucinda, I have to go—someone at the door. I'll speak to you again. Bye.'

She almost dropped the phone, her fingers were shaking so badly. It was a funny thing, until today it hadn't really seemed real, but with seeing Jan and Ben together, and her grandmother mentioning the wedding, suddenly it seemed not only real but terribly, terribly close.

She made a cup of coffee and ran a bath, and then discovered that she wouldn't, after all, be having Ben's baby, so she chucked the coffee down the sink, poured herself a glass of cooking sherry and sat in the bath sipping it and watching the tears drip into the water until she decided she'd been silly enough for one night.

She didn't really want the sherry anyway, and the last thing she needed was a hangover—or Ben's baby to bring up on her own, so it was silly to cry because she couldn't have what she didn't want, she told herself firmly.

She climbed out of the tepid water, towelled herself briskly dry and curled up in front of the gas fire to watch the nth rerun of an American cop series before going to bed.

The following week was hell.

Maggie thought she was faring badly, but when she saw Ben she was shocked at how drawn he looked. He was thinner, and his eyes were shadowed and hollow-looking.

He hardly spoke to her, even when necessary, and whenever he followed up a child it always seemed to be in her absence.

Little David Wise, the boy with epiglottitis, had made an excellent recovery and been discharged home, and Stephen Phillips had settled on his insulin and was expected to return home for a long weekend and see how the family managed.

The nurses had been teaching him how to inject himself, and he was coping very bravely with the endless finger-pricks for the Clinistix tests, probably the hardest and most unpleasant part of the whole business.

Maggie wanted to share it with Ben, but there was no way the lines of communication were that far open any longer, and Jo was too busy planning her holiday to listen.

Anne Gabriel, whose daughter Beth was nearly seven, was more inclined to listen, but too busy with the cases Alex had brought forward to have much time.

And every day the wedding drew closer.

At least she now had her car back so she could get to and from work without relying on the sporadic bus service, but it was just as well she did because she ended up working late in the evening on Tuesday and Wednesday.

On Thursday Lucinda rang.

'Darling, I want you to have dinner with me on Saturday evening,' she said. 'I've got something simply wonderful to tell you, and you absolutely have to come.'

'Oh, Grannie,' Maggie began, 'I really don't think I'll feel like it——'

'Nonsense! Darling, you must! I'll never forgive you if you don't.'

'Well, then, I won't come, and we'll be quits,' she said crossly.

Lucinda tutted at her. 'That really wasn't very nice——'

'It wasn't meant to be.'

'Please? For me?'

Maggie sighed. 'Oh, all right then. What time?'

'Eight—at the Country Club.'

'What? Oh, no. I can cope with supper at your house——'

'Well, I can't! I will have been at the wedding all day and my feet'll be killing me. The last thing I'm going to do is cook. No, my darling, I simply insist.'

Maggie hadn't known her grandmother for twenty-eight years without knowing when to give in. With a resigned sigh she agreed, and, after a few moments of general chatter, she said goodbye.

Friday was busier than usual, a fact for which she was profoundly grateful. She really didn't want time to think about Ben. When she was called down to A and E, it was by Jim Harris, the consultant, and Ben was nowhere to be seen.

Kathleen was, however, and told her that Ben had left for the day.

'He's a lot of preparations to make for tomorrow, and needed the time,' she explained, and Maggie nodded miserably.

'Do you know, Maggie, he's been a tower of strength?' Kathleen went on. 'The way he dealt with that boy with epiglottitis, and that little girl with osteogenesis imperfecta—you know, she came in with her mother and he took me aside instantly and told me what was the matter. "She's deaf," he said, "and look at the whites of her eyes". Sharp as a tack, he is. Everyone else had missed it for years!'

So he hadn't stolen her diagnosis after all. Maggie felt guilty for doubting him, although at the time it had seemed quite reasonable because she was cross with him for countless other transgressions.

Perhaps she hadn't misjudged him at all? After all, Jan had arrived out of the blue and announced that they were getting married. What if he had changed his mind, but was too much of a gentleman to let Jan down, having proposed to her in the past? Perhaps he'd been proposing to her as a matter of routine for so long it had just become habit?

Whatever, he was marrying her tomorrow, and Maggie—Maggie was not.

She busied herself with the notes for the child just admitted, and then made her way back to the ward.

On the way she bumped into Jo Carter.

'Oh, Maggie—could you do us a favour while we're away? Would you water the plants, love?'

'Of course—that's fine.'

'Are you sure you don't mind? I'd ask Annie, but she's going to be even busier while we're away, and she needs to spend what little free time she has with Beth.'

'That's OK. I really don't mind, I'll be happy to.'

'Great!' Jo's lovely face lit up. 'Only one more hurdle to go, and we can get away—we're having difficulty tracking down the person who's covering me. He's an old friend, and he was due back in the country yesterday, but there's no sign of him. I hope to goodness he turns up. Would you pop round this evening so we can show you how to work the burglar alarm and give you a key?'

She nodded. 'Fine—what time?'

Jo shrugged. 'Seven-thirty? Have something to eat with us.'

Maggie shook her head. 'No, I'll come round but I won't eat with you—I'm not very good company.'

'Rubbish! I'll expect you at seven-thirty, on the dot, hungry.'

Maggie laughed. 'You have a lot in common with my grandmother,' she told Jo.

'I'm not sure that was meant to be a compliment,' Jo said wryly. 'I must dash—I'll see you later.'

It was a bit of a rush to get there on time, but Maggie almost managed it.

'I was being sent to get you,' Alex said as he opened the door.

She laughed. 'Sorry I'm a bit late—things were on the drag at the hospital.'

He rolled his eyes. 'Now there's an unusual occurrence. Come on in—Jo's on the phone and I'm supposed to be stirring the chilli. Can I get you a drink?'

She followed him to the kitchen and frowned doubtfully at the bottle of wine he offered her. 'I don't think so—well, something soft, perhaps? Alcohol and I don't agree awfully well.'

Alex chuckled. 'I heard about the party—are you still being teased?'

'Only by the husbands of friends,' she said wryly.

He apologised—with a definite twinkle lurking in his eye!—and handed her a glass of Perrier with a slice of lemon.

Then Jo arrived. 'Sorry about that—I was talking to Barbara about Amy.'

'How is she—any news?'

'Oh, she's fine,' Jo said with a sigh, and flopped into a chair, running her fingers through her wild mane. 'I just wish. . .'

'"If wishes were horses",' Maggie said quietly, and Jo smiled understandingly at her.

'Big day tomorrow—are you sure you'll be all right? I worry about you on your own. Alex, could we hang on and go on Sunday?'

'We may have to anyway if your friend doesn't turn up, so yes, of course we can hang on.'

'Don't be daft!' Maggie said emphatically. 'You need your holiday—I'll be fine. I'm going to Norwich to spend the balance of my grandmother's Christmas present on some exotic clothes, and then I'm going out to dinner with her tomorrow night—I've even got the pearls out of the bank to wear. Call it defiance if you like, but he wouldn't take them back, and I'll have to sell them, so I might as well wear them one last time.'

'Absolutely right,' Alex said cheerfully. 'If the man's damn fool enough to squander thousands of pounds on you, you might as well give in grace-fully—not that you don't deserve it, of course!'

'Of course,' Maggie said drily, and they all laughed.

He dished up the chilli—a vegetarian recipe in deference to Jo—and, as they ate it in the kitchen round the breakfast table, Maggie thought what a lovely man he was and how fortunate Jo was to have met him. She was a very complex and deeply thoughtful person, and he seemed to understand her moods and feelings almost intuitively.

There had been a time when Maggie had thought she and Ben could have had something like that, but how wrong she had been!

She dragged her attention back to the conversation, and when they had finished the meal they cleared the table and then Jo gave her a guided tour of the plants.

'There are thousands!' Maggie said with a laugh.

'No, just hundreds,' Alex corrected. 'Jo, there's a BMW on the drive—anyone you know?'

'No—unless——'

Just then the doorbell rang and Jo ran down the hall and flung open the front door.

'Jake!'

The man standing in the doorway looked travel-stained and weary, but his brown eyes above the heavily stubbled chin held the warmth of love, and with a glad cry Jo threw herself into his arms. Maggie blinked and glanced at Alex. He was smiling broadly, so this was obviously not a visitor he considered a threat to the status quo.

The man put Jo down and held her at arm's length.

'You're looking good, Jo-Jo—really good,' he said, and his voice was filled with pride. He turned to Alex, extending his hand and a smile of greeting. 'You must be the lucky man—good to meet you.'

'And you—I can't tell you how pleased we are to see you, Jake. Our holiday was about to be abandoned!'

Jake laughed. 'Sorry about that. The phone lines from eastern Europe are a touch on the iffy side at the moment, and I couldn't get a message to you. God, what a journey! Anyway, I'm here, and I'm starving. I suppose you've eaten?'

'There's always been food in my fridge for you, Jake,' Jo told him laughingly. 'Just hold your horses a minute until you've met Maggie—she's a paediatrician and you'll be working with her from Monday.'

He shook Maggie's hand, his grip warm and firm, and Maggie thought again what an open and friendly person he was.

'You'll also be working with Annie, of course,' Jo put in, almost as an afterthought.

Jake's attention snapped back to her instantly.

'Annie? Anne Gabriel?'

'Did I forget to mention it?' Jo said innocently.

'You certainly did—Annie, here? God, I haven't seen her in—oh, years! How is she—and how's the child? She must be five or six by now.'

'Nearly seven. She's fine—she's a lovely little girl.'

Jake's face was a study of conflicting emotions. 'It'll be good to see them—so how did Annie end up here?'

'A little engineering by yours truly,' Jo said with a smug smile. 'I like having my friends around me.'

'She's my SHO,' Alex told him, 'and a damn fine doctor. If maternity hadn't carved a hole in her career, she'd be doing really well by now. She'll be a great help to you.'

The conversation was obviously set to go on all night, and Maggie felt distinctly *de trop*. 'Look, you've obviously got a lot to talk about,' she said. 'I'll go and leave you to it, if you can just show me the burglar alarm.'

Jo kissed her goodbye. 'All the best for tomorrow, Maggie. I'll be thinking of you.'

Alex gave her a key, demonstrated the workings of the alarm and waved her off.

As she drove home, she thought of Jake and Jo and Anne—obviously old college friends. And she thought of something Annie had said about a wild night with an old friend. Surely not?

And yet he had seemed somehow familiar. . .

A car shot out of a side turning and forced her to swerve, and so she put idle speculation out of her mind and concentrated on getting home safely.

She made an early start to Norwich in the morning, and, firmly dismissing all thoughts of the wedding, she found a lovely skirt, three blouses and a jumper which were practical but very good quality and would last her well.

So much for common sense. Remembering her dinner date with Lucinda and her vow to get something outrageous, she found herself looking through clothes in a fashionable little shop in a side-street.

'Did you have anything particular in mind, madam?' the assistant asked her.

'Well, not—something for tonight. I'm having dinner in a country club with my grandmother.'

'Something fairly demure, then?'

Maggie laughed. 'No, not at all. My grandmother is possibly the most outrageous person I know, and it's her money. I think I ought to spend it as she would!'

The assistant smiled. 'Any jewellery, in particular?'

'Oh—yes, pearls.'

'And will your hair be up or down?'

'Up?'

'I think so. Right, let's have a look.'

There followed an endless stream of dresses, until finally the assistant handed her one and smiled. 'This one, I think.'

Maggie stared doubtfully at the dark blue and gold shot-silk taffeta gown. 'But it's strapless! It'll fall down!'

'Nonsense! It's boned—try it on, it really is just your colour.'

'Yes—it'll go with the bags under my eyes,' Maggie said ruefully, but she pulled it on anyway,

and twisted her hair up into a knot, holding it on top
of her head with one hand.

'Oh—that is really very special on you, you
know,' the assistant said.

Maggie was stunned. It did look special—very
special. She would have loved to wear it for Ben. . .

'I'll take it.'

She dropped her hair, tugged down the zip and
handed the dress to the assistant. It had just dawned
on her that he would be married by now, and she
had to get out of the shop before she disgraced
herself.

Grabbing her parcels, she paid the assistant and
fled, running back to the car and driving as quickly
as she dared out of Norwich and in the direction of
the Broads.

She had lunch in a pub overlooking the river, and
hoped that if anyone saw her they would think she
had smoke in her eyes. She mustn't think about
him—not today, not ever again.

After a while the atmosphere became too much,
and she left the pub and walked along the riverbank
until she was exhausted.

Her watch said four o'clock and the light was
almost gone by the time she returned to the car.

The wedding would be over now, all the guests
going home, and Ben—Ben was forever out of
reach.

Drained of emotion, Maggie started her car and
drove quietly home.

Only pride prevented her from cancelling her dinner
date with her grandmother—pride and the fact that

she couldn't bear to spend the evening alone sitting thinking about what Ben might be doing.

It was pride too that made her take extra care with her appearance, and when she arrived at the country club a few minutes early and walked into the crowded foyer she was glad she had made the effort.

She made her way to the desk, conscious of the turning heads that followed her progress, and told the receptionist that she was meeting Mrs Wells for dinner.

'I believe she has made a reservation?'

'Oh, yes, Dr Wells, your companion hasn't arrived yet. If you'd like to take a seat in the lounge bar one of the waiters will bring you a drink while you wait.'

'Thank you.'

She found a table in the corner and sat facing the room watching the glittering crowd and sipping her mineral water. She could have done with some Dutch courage before having to listen to Lucinda rabbiting on about the wedding, but she was driving and her sense of responsibility outweighed her dread—marginally.

Suddenly her eye was caught by a familiar figure, immaculate in evening dress, his fair hair gleaming gold in the lamplight.

As he turned towards her, his eyes met hers and held, and Maggie felt an overwhelming need to run.

What was he doing here? And where was Jan? Oh, God, they couldn't be spending their wedding night here, could they?

And then it was too late to run because he was standing beside her, his smile strained.

'Hello, Maggie,' he said quietly.

'What are you doing here?' she asked, her voice taut with emotion.

'Meeting my stepfather—what about you?'

'My grandmother—she isn't here yet.'

'Nor's Gerald.' He gave a brief, humourless laugh. 'I think, my dear, we've been set up.'

CHAPTER TEN

'I-I DON'T understand! How have we been set up?'

'May I?'

Ben indicated a chair, and Maggie nodded distractedly. 'Of course. Ben, I really don't know what you're talking about. . .'

'Matchmaking.'

'*What*? But what about the wedding?'

He shrugged. 'You weren't there.'

Maggie frowned and wondered what she'd missed. 'I feel like Alice—I think I've fallen down a rabbit hole here,' she said. 'Could you explain—where's Jan?'

He glanced at his watch. 'Probably somewhere over the Atlantic by now, on the way to Florida.'

'But why aren't you with her?'

Ben laughed. 'Why in the hell should I be with her? She doesn't want me on her honeymoon, and I would think Robert would have something to say about it, too!'

Maggie was getting more and more confused. 'Robert?'

'Her husband of eight hours—Maggie, are you OK?'

She shook her head to clear it. 'Robert is Jan's husband?'

He nodded. 'Yes. Of course he is.'

'But she married you.'

It was his turn to look confused. 'What?'

Maggie took a deep swallow of her mineral water, wished again that it was stronger and set it down on the table.

'Let's start from the beginning. Who's Jan?'

'My stepsister—but surely you knew that?'

'But on the ship, she said you were getting married——'

'Hang on. On the ship?'

She nodded miserably. 'That last morning. I came to say goodbye, and caught you with her in your arms, making wedding plans.'

'Her wedding plans. Not mine.'

Maggie stared at him, unable to believe the flicker of hope that danced just out of reach.

'So you didn't marry her today?'

'No—of course not. She's my stepsister—hold on. Is that what this is all about? Why you had this sudden change of heart and wouldn't let me near you?'

Maggie nodded. 'I thought you'd been in love with her all along and were just passing time with me and the others.'

'Others? What others?'

'Oh, that creature in tinsel on New Year's Eve——'

'New Year's Eve? I was with you on New Year's Eve—or I was until Ah Seng called me away to deal with Vic Matthews.'

Maggie sighed. 'But I saw her, Ben, coming away from the medical centre in the morning, still dressed in that ridiculous outfit——'

Ben started to laugh.

'It isn't funny! I happen to think fidelity is very important, and one minute you were about to make

love to me, and the next that—that *vile* tart was
leaving your cabin still dressed in the previous
night's clothes, and you laugh about it!'

Seeing Maggie's obvious distress, Ben sobered a
little and took her hand. 'Oh, my darling—shall I
tell you what she was doing coming out of the
medical centre—not my cabin, please note? She
came to me that morning complaining of pains in the
chest, and insisted I examined her carefully—very
carefully. I told her that if she was experiencing
discomfort she ought to discuss it with her plastic
surgeon. She was most upset with me.'

Maggie felt a reluctant smile touch her lips. 'And
that's all?'

He nodded. 'That's all—nothing else, I promise.
How could you think, even for a minute, that that
promiscuous little tart was my type?'

'You didn't come back,' Maggie said quietly. 'I
waited hours for you.'

He took her hand. 'I was busy. Vic Matthews was
very ill. I was worried about him, and then the
others started to complain of similar things, and I
didn't know what to think. I told you all that at the
time.'

She nodded unhappily. 'And I believed you—
then. It was only later, when I'd seen you with Jan,
that I thought about tinsel-toes again and wondered
if you'd told me the truth.'

A waiter came up to them and told them their
table was ready.

Ben turned to her and shrugged. 'Shall we eat?'

Maggie smiled. 'We might as well—I take it
they're paying?'

Ben laughed. 'Oh, yes, one way or the other!'

The waiter looked a little bemused but showed them to their table with elaborate courtesy.

It was tucked away in a little alcove, screened by plants, softly lit and with a single red rose in a vase on the table.

The setting was so unashamedly romantic that Maggie felt suddenly shy.

She looked up and met Ben's eyes, and they were heavy with desire.

'Have I told you how beautiful you look this evening?' he murmured.

She flushed and dropped her eyes to her lap. 'Thank you.'

'You're wearing the pearls.'

Her hand came up and lay against them. They seemed to glow with warmth.

'I decided to wear them one last time. I was going to sell them.'

'And now? Where do we go from here, Maggie?'

She looked away. So many terrible things had been said on both sides. Could they ever be forgiven?

'Can we take it one step at a time?'

'Of course.'

The waiter reappeared discreetly and took their order, and Maggie toyed with her food and followed Ben's lead in the conversation.

He told her that the shipping line was refunding all the passengers in full, and claiming off the hotel chain for damages.

'You'll be getting a refund and a complimentary cruise for your help during the epidemic.'

She frowned. 'How do you know?'

A small smile played around his mouth. 'Gerald

owns the shipping line. That was how I knew the vacancy existed. It's a job with a fairly rapid turn-over, and it just seemed like the ideal opportunity to get right away and think about what I wanted and what I was doing.'

'And have you had enough time to decide?'

'Oh, yes. I was bored to tears within a few weeks—but then you guessed that. When Bron's job came up, Gerald suggested I should take it, at least temporarily, and by then I'd been on the ship long enough to be ripping my hair out for some action. Then Vic Matthews arrested, and for a few seconds my confidence just deserted me.'

He smiled wryly. 'Then you yelled at me, and it all just fell into place. I had no right to make decisions about his life for him—that's between him and God, if you like. We're just there, to serve the public, to push necessary buttons. They need to know they can trust us to do that, and, in A and E, at least, ethics don't really enter into it. It's just a case of moving fast and doing the best you can, and I love it. I like being on the sharp end. I just needed to clarify my own feelings about some of the pro-cedures. Now I've done that, I can get on with my life, and I'm really very happy there.'

Maggie poked her salmon trout with a fork. 'Kathleen seems very taken with you.'

'Kathleen? She's a marvellous sister, wonderful to work with.'

'I saw her getting in your car.'

'I gave her a lift home.'

'You gave me a lift home, and look what happened.'

He laid down his fork and gazed at her sadly. 'Don't you trust me at all?'

She looked away, unable to meet his eyes, and then looked back. 'I would like to. . .'

'Please do. Apart from you there hasn't been anybody for ages—not since before the court case. Oh, I've had flirtations, but you're the only person I've taken to bed in about eighteen months—and I was never promiscuous.'

She searched his face, and knew he was telling her the truth. A slow smile broke out on her lips. 'Of course I trust you. I'm sorry I didn't. It didn't fit with what I thought I knew of you, but some of the things you said. . .'

He gripped her hand. 'I wish I'd never given you those damn pearls. They've caused so much pain.'

He pushed his plate away and looked up again, his face serious. A muscle twitched in his jaw, and he swallowed.

'Tell me,' he said eventually. 'When you said you could never love me——'

'I was lying. I think I've loved you since the night we met.'

His eyes closed briefly. 'Oh, God, Maggie, I was almost afraid to ask! I didn't dare to hope that you might feel the same. When I took you out on deck that first night and kissed you, I was sure you were going to throw me overboard or have me keel-hauled for my impertinence, and then the next night—I came so close to making love to you there on the deck under the stars.'

She smiled at the memory. 'I wouldn't have minded.'

'And now?'

His voice was deep and husky with emotion.

'Now?'

'I want to hold you, Maggie, and make love to you all night—I've missed you so much. The nights have been so lonely without you.'

'Oh, Ben. . .'

He stood up abruptly. 'Come on, let's get out of here.'

He held her chair and led her through to the reception area, but there they were greeted with a scene of confusion.

'Good God, it's snowing—look!'

They could see the car park through the glass doors, and in the floodlights the snow swirled in a blinding mass.

'We'd better wait till it stops,' Maggie suggested.

'We could always stay the night.'

She met his eyes, and her heart crashed against her ribs. 'We haven't got any luggage,' she whispered.

'So what? We've got the ideal excuse.' He leant over the desk to the beleaguered receptionist. 'The name's Bradshaw—do you have a room available tonight?'

'No, I'm sorry, sir, we're fully—— Did you say Dr Bradshaw?'

'That's right.'

She reached under the desk. 'Was that one room or two, sir?'

'One—double.'

She smiled, her expression carefully schooled. 'There is a reservation for you and Dr Wells—Suite twenty-one. Will that be all right?'

Ben's lips twitched. 'Yes, that'll be fine.'

She lifted down a key and summoned a porter to show them to their room.

'There you are, sir,' he said, opening the door with a flourish. 'Would you like me to open the champagne for you?'

'Champagne?' Maggie squeaked.

'Thank you, no, I can manage.'

He tipped the man heavily, and as the door closed behind him Ben shrugged off his dinner-jacket and dropped it on to the arm of the little settee.

There was an ice-bucket with a bottle of vintage champagne on the coffee-table, and an envelope was tucked under it.

Ben removed it and slit it open, pulling out the note.

'"If you've got this far, presumably congratulations are in order, and about time too. All our very best love, Lucinda and Gerald."' Ben snorted and dropped the note on the coffee-table. 'A little previous; I don't know if you'll have me yet.'

Maggie smiled softly. 'Oh, I think you could take a gamble and open the bottle.'

Ben met her eyes, his own racked with doubt. 'You said in Singapore that it was going to take you a lifetime to pay for the pearls—if I start now, do you think by the time we're old and grey I'll be able to earn your forgiveness for the terrible things I've said to you?'

'Oh, Ben, there's nothing to forgive,' Maggie told him gently. 'At least when I thought you were marrying Jan I had a reason to be so unkind to you—you can't have known what was going on. I must have seemed a real tease.'

'I could have killed O'Shea at that party.'

'It was my fault.'

'No—no, my love, it was my fault. Your virginity was the most precious gift I've ever been given. I had no right to put a price on it, but it was only when I said I'd overlook the next fifty years that it dawned on me what I'd lost.'

'You haven't lost me, Ben. I'm still here, and if you want me I always will be.'

Then she was in his arms and he was raining kisses on her face, his fingers cradling her cheeks while he murmured words of love against her skin.

'Take me to bed,' she whispered, and he led her through to the bedroom and undressed her slowly, his eyes tracking hotly over her skin.

When she reached for his bow-tie, he shook his head.

'Too slow,' he told her, and stripped rapidly, tearing off buttons in his haste. While he fought with his clothes she threw back the covers and climbed up and knelt in the middle of the high four-poster bed, watching him while she lifted her hands to take down her hair.

'No—let me.'

He joined her, kneeling facing her, his thighs around hers, and, reaching up, he pulled out the pins securing her hair.

It tumbled round her shoulders and he ran his hands through it, spreading it like spun silk over her skin.

'My beautiful mermaid,' he whispered huskily, and, winding his fingers into her hair, he drew her towards him until their bodies were touching.

Her breath caught in her throat, and she laid her

hands on his chest, feeling the pounding of his heart beneath her palms.

'Marry me, Maggie—stay with me forever.'

'Oh, Ben, yes—forever.'

He claimed her then, his touch gentle but possessive, and she claimed him too, wild and demanding until at last, slaked with passion, they lay together side by side and slept.

Maggie woke to the feeling of Ben's finger tracing the outline of her lips.

'That tickles,' she complained gently.

'Sorry.' He bent and kissed her instead. 'Better?'

'Mmm. Ben, will you tell me something?'

'Yes, of course, if I know the answer.'

She propped herself up on one elbow and looked him in the eye. 'How much were the pearls?'

He groaned. 'That's a lousy thing to do to me.'

'Tell.'

'No.'

'You promised.'

'I was expecting some inquisition about my past love-life, not a checking of our mutual assets.'

She blinked. 'Do we have mutual assets? Apart from the pearls and your horribly ostentatious car?'

He snorted. 'My car is a nice car.'

'No, it isn't, it's a bachelor's girl-catcher. Answer the question.'

'Yes, we have mutual assets.'

'Such as?'

'Half the shipping line. My father and Gerald were partners. My father's half was left in trust for me.'

'Good grief! Are you telling me you're rich?'

He smiled. 'I suppose I am, to an extent. I don't have to work, let's put it like that.'

'So how much were they?'

He groaned. 'Are we back to that?'

'Thousands?'

'Yes.'

'More or less than five?'

'You talk too much.'

'Answer me.'

'No, it's irrelevant.'

'Not to me it isn't—oh! What are you doing?'

'What do you think I'm doing?'

She giggled. 'That's naughty.'

'No it isn't, you're almost my wife. Be quiet.'

'I'm not going to promise to obey you in the marriage service, you know.'

He laughed. 'That's nothing less than I'd expected. I shall have to find a way of ensuring your co-operation.'

She gasped.

'Have I found it?'

She gasped again.

'I believe I have. You're speechless!'

'Shut up and make love to me, please,' she told him breathlessly.

'My pleasure.'

He took her in his arms and cradled her against his chest with a sigh. 'In a little while, when we can be bothered, we ought to ring Lucinda and Gerald and tell them their plan worked.'

Maggie laughed. 'Let them sweat for a while— we'll ring them tomorrow evening.'

'Good idea.'

He lowered his head and kissed her.

'I love you, Maggie,' he said softly. 'Let's get married soon. I really don't want to wait.'

'We have to wait two weeks for Jo and Alex to get back.'

He sighed. 'I suppose we ought to wait for Jan and Robert, too, but I really don't want to. Can't we just sneak off and get married and then have a party for everybody else later?'

'How tempting. I tell you what, if Lucinda gets wind of it before the deed is done we'll have no say in the decision-making.'

'That does it,' he said firmly. 'We'll get a special licence and get married as soon as possible without telling a soul. After today, I really couldn't stand a big, fussy wedding.'

'Lucinda will say she's been cheated, and, after all, if it hadn't been for her, we wouldn't be here like this now.'

He laughed. 'No, I would have met you in the normal way in the hospital, and I would have fallen head over heels in love with you and you wouldn't have overheard Jan on the ship and we would probably be in bed in my flat now instead of here.'

Maggie smiled. 'I enjoyed the cruise, and it is a nice bed.'

Ben sighed and flopped back on to the mattress. 'Do I take it you want a big, elaborate wedding?'

'I wouldn't mind,' she said wistfully. 'Would you hate it?'

'Not really, I suppose, but I want to be with you,' he said frankly.

She sat up and looked down at him. 'Well, we don't have to be apart until then, do we?'

'Yes we do. I'm old-fashioned, Maggie. I'm not

living with you until we're married, and I'm not creeping around in the middle of the night sneaking kisses, either.'

'How about—Wednesday?'

He laughed. 'Make it two weeks, so Jan and Robert and Jo and Alex can come, and I'll make do with sneaking around just a little.'

Maggie chuckled. 'You wanna sneak around now, mister?'

He reached up and pulled her down on to his chest. 'Wicked woman.'

'Only with you—only ever with you.'

'Oh, Maggie. . .'

His lips found hers in a kiss of profound tenderness that rapidly spiralled into a white-hot passion that only a lifetime together would assuage. Then together they slept, their limbs entwined, until the thin rays of the winter sun crawled over the horizon and turned the snow to gold.

The last book in the trilogy comes next month. Look for Annie's story, KNAVE OF HEARTS, when Jake unexpectedly returns. . .

Love is in the Air...

Mills & Boon have commissioned four of your favourite authors to write four tender romances.

Guaranteed love and excitement for St. Valentine's Day

A BRILLIANT DISGUISE	-	Rosalie Ash
FLOATING ON AIR	-	Angela Devine
THE PROPOSAL	-	Betty Neels
VIOLETS ARE BLUE	-	Jennifer Taylor

Available from January 1993   PRICE £3.99

_Available from Boots, Martins, John Menzies, W.H. Smith,
most supermarkets and other paperback stockists.
Also available from Mills & Boon Reader Service, PO Box 236,
Thornton Road, Croydon, Surrey CR9 3RU._

Mills & Boon

Discover the thrill of 4 Exciting Medical Romances – FREE

BOOKS FOR YOU

In the exciting world of modern medicine, the emotions of true love have an added drama. Now you can experience four of these unforgettable romantic tales of passion and heartbreak FREE – and look forward to a regular supply of Mills & Boon Medical Romances delivered direct to your door!

❧ ❧ ❧

Turn the page for details of 2 extra free gifts, and how to apply.

An Irrcsistible Offer from Mills & Boon

Here's an offer from Mills & Boon to become a regular reader of Medical Romances. To welcome you, we'd like you to have four books, a cuddly teddy and a special MYSTERY GIFT, all absolutely free and without obligation.

Then, every month you could look forward to receiving 4 more **brand new** Medical Romances for £1.70 each, delivered direct to your door, post and packing free. Plus our newsletter featuring author news, competitions, special offers, and lots more.

This invitation comes with no strings attached. You can cancel or suspend your subscription at any time, and still keep your free books and gifts.

Its so easy. Send no money now. Simply fill in the coupon below and post it at once to -

**Mills & Boon Reader Service, FREEPOST,
PO Box 236, Croydon, Surrey CR9 9EL**

NO STAMP REQUIRED

YES! Please rush me my 4 Free Medical Romances and 2 Free Gifts! Please also reserve me a Reader Service Subscription. If I decide to subscribe, I can look forward to receiving 4 brand new Medical Romances every month for just £6.80, delivered direct to my door. Post and packing is free, and there's a free Mills & Boon Newsletter. If I choose not to subscribe I shall write to you within 10 days - I can keep the books and gifts whatever I decide. I can cancel or suspend my subscription at any time. I am over 18.

EP20D

Name (Mr/Mrs/Ms) _____

Address _____

_____ Postcode _____

Signature_____

mps
MAILING
PREFERENCE
SERVICE